pirogue wipeout

The Big Uneasy Book 7

pauline baird jones

Copyright © 2022 by Pauline Baird Jones

All rights reserved.

No part of this book may be reproduced in any form or by any electronic or mechanical means, including information storage and retrieval systems, without written permission from the author, except for the use of brief quotations in a book review.

ISBN: 9798352539538

❦ Created with Vellum

about pirogue wipe out

No one is going to get what they want this time.

No-nonsense Coast Guard agent, Dan Baker finds himself going where he doesn't want to go (the swamp) and feeling what he never thought he'd feel (in love or in like). He really hopes the mysterious Gemma isn't the murderer because he doesn't want or need her in his life.

Gemma Bailey's "get away from it all" summer on the charter boat *Reel Escape*, is not turning out like she'd hoped. There is a dubious lawyer, a sinister mob figure, and some murders. Was it the Rougarou? It is a pity the way too attractive Dan Baker thinks she's the murderer.

Can they untwist the tangled ties, clear Gemma and the Rougarou, and ride off into the sunset on Dan's Triumph?

Don't miss out on this latest installment in the Big Uneasy series!

pirogue noun

pi·rogue | \ 'pē-ˌrōg

The term 'pirogue' does not refer to a specific kind of boat, but it is a generic term in Louisiana for small canoes, flat boats, or shallow draft boats for navigating the swamps.

It's also fun to say. 😊

chapter one

It was stinking hot.

And it stinking stank.

The swamp was not Special Agent Dan Baker's favorite place to be in September—or most other months of the year. He wasn't a fan of the critters or creatures who did like the swamp. And even when it wasn't totally stinking hot, it always stank.

He flashed his ID in unison with his partner, Ruth Fossette, and they clambered out of the air boat onto a dock—one that already seemed too crowded with local law enforcement.

It didn't look like it could hold another person, but somehow managed two more.

He might have held his breath for his first step or two. It creaked and swayed but didn't collapse. That was good. The water under the dock was not the kind to cool you down. It would just stink you up—not to mention putting you in biting distance of any gators hanging around.

As they passed by the LEOs, he studied the hunting camp at the end of the dock. It looked as neglected as the dock, but it fit right into the swamp.

Dan jumped a gap where a couple of the boards had rotted away and kept going. It didn't seem like a good place to ponder the odds on how much weight the boards on the other side would take.

The local LEO's either smirked or looked confused at the sight of their IDs.

The CGIS—the Coast Guard Investigative Service—wasn't that well known, even within law enforcement circles.

Dan could privately admit he hadn't known that much about CGIS, and he'd been with the Coast Guard's Search and Rescue for years before transferring over a year ago.

Ruth had recruited him hard before he gave in—her persuasions helped by a broken leg during a particularly tricky rescue.

He was getting too old for crap like that.

He hadn't missed SAR as much as he thought he would. There had been plenty of excitement of a different kind and—he hated to admit it—he'd liked the mental challenge of solving crimes. Wearing civvies again was also a plus.

"Took you long enough," was all Ruth had said when he told her.

Somehow, without him saying it, she'd known why he'd resisted for so long.

He'd joined the Coast Guard to get as far away from his family law enforcement legacy as he could, without fighting the family's serve-and-protect genes.

Ruth also seemed to know that he hadn't told his family about the transfer. That Ruth had persuaded him to circle back into the family legacy—and that he liked it—did not make him ready to face a myriad of "told you so's" from his siblings and his dad. Especially his dad. Zach's favorite thing was to, "I told you so," his kids.

"You can't hide it forever," she'd pointed out just this morning, when she'd met him not far from their airboat ride. He'd parked his Triumph Bonneville, switched his leather jacket for a sport jacket, and locked his rig down.

As they walked over to their airboat, he might have glanced

around to make sure no family was around. They had a habit of popping up in unexpected places.

"I plan to tell them next time I'm up in New Orleans." He knew he sounded defensive for a forty-five-year old man who had a right to live his own life.

"You said that last time," she pointed out laconically.

"Things were weird."

"Things are always weird with your family."

It was true. He had a sister-in-law who was related to two mob families. One of his sisters performed autopsies for Orleans parish, one was a crime scene investigator, and another was an EMT. Cops, a firefighter, a lawyer—he even had a brother who was "just" a PI, who had managed to get himself shot at and married last month.

They pretty much had things covered if something went wrong—which it often did.

Just the fact that there were thirteen of them was weird, his dad's Baker's dozen.

"You should come up and see Gideon's fake classic Peugeot before they sell it," Dan said. How the "Columbo" car had been acquired was a story he had yet to hear.

When you had six brothers and six sisters, quiet chats—and hard information—were difficult to come by. And it was dangerous to dig into others' secrets when he was keeping a secret that kept getting harder to spill as each day went by.

He might, he made an internal face, be a touch proud he'd managed to keep it under the radar for so long. He might have broken the sibling secrets' record.

Ruth's brows had arched higher than usual "I'd like to hear that story."

"So would I." He might be surprised he hadn't run into Gideon, since he kept his boat moored in a berth close by. But he'd also just gotten married. So maybe he wasn't that surprised.

He'd shook the siblings thoughts off like a dog after a bath and looked at Ruth.

"So what's the deal?" He'd asked to change the subject and because he did want to know where they were going. As they settled in the airboat, he pulled out his phone to go over the information he'd been sent.

"Local LEOs found a body at a remote hunting camp. Initial ID is that he was Coast Guard."

Which made the body their problem. Sometimes local law enforcement cared about jurisdiction and sometimes they didn't. When it was this hot? They didn't as much.

Dan frowned. "I hadn't heard of any of our guys going missing?"

He pulled up the file and frowned. "This says he's already dead."

"If you keep reading, you'll find that he went missing when he was a passenger on a small plane thirty-five years ago. The pilot filed a flight plan from Tampa to New Orleans, but it never arrived. He was declared dead, but the body was never found."

He looked up with a frown. "So we have a thirty-five year old corpse? How did they ID him so fast?"

Ruth shook her head. "Fingerprints."

Dan started to object. There wouldn't be fingerprints if he died thirty-five years ago. When the swamp was involved, it didn't take long to erase all but the bones. So their guy hadn't died thirty-five years ago. Missing didn't always mean dead.

Their driver fired up the engine and it became impossible to talk, so he went back to reading the data packet their team had put together for them.

There had been searches, but it had been a large search area. He knew what that was like. But now that the missing man had turned up, it seemed like the plane had been ditched on purpose.

He made a note for the team to look at events around the time of the disappearance. If someone went missing and stayed missing, they usually had a compelling reason.

He frowned as he read on. There'd been another passenger, but she'd never been identified. How did they know she—oh, witnesses in Tampa insisted they'd seen a woman board the plane, too.

They'd never been able to link the unknown woman to any missing persons reports.

Conspiracy theorists had gotten onboard and over the years there had been so-called sightings of the plane, prompting a flurry of searches.

Nothing had ever been found.

The engine shut off, yanking him back to the present and their nasty crime scene.

"You coming?" Ruth asked.

He didn't want to. He could already smell the decomposition of the body and they were still several yards from the cabin.

The concentrated heat inside would boost the stench factor by a number he'd rather not know.

"I should never have let you talk me into this," Dan said as he followed her in.

* * *

It was September in southern Louisiana, but muggy was hanging on with serious intent to cause misery as long as it could.

It was a good thing that Gemma Bailey knew how far to lower her expectations, even though this part of Louisiana was new to her. When she'd crewed for her dad on the *Reel Escape*, they mostly hung around the Florida coast.

Now that he was gone, his co-owner and partner, Little Abner Abbot, had apparently decided to expand further along the Gulf Coast. Or his charter had persuaded him?

Gemma eased her cellphone a little further from her ear, in hopes of catching a random breeze off the bayou.

"That sounds perfect, Sarah," Gemma said. "I'll keep an eye out for your guy, but I don't think he'll have trouble finding us."

She could see the highway from where she stood on the fly deck as they made their way up the bayou.

She rang off and turned as Little Abner joined her.

"That was Blue Bayou Catering," she said, giving him a smile while trying not to notice how old he looked this summer. "Our charter will have his *special* meal for his *special* guest. It's coming by *special* courier not long after we dock."

"Which Blaine is paying for?" It wasn't really a question and Little Abner wasn't little. He was pushing 70 and a crusty stereotype of an old sea dog, but underestimate him at your peril. It might be a cliche, but he was as shrewd as the day was long.

When her dad passed away last year, she'd inherited his share of the *Reel Escape*, but it wasn't like she could sail off with her half. Little Abner couldn't afford to buy her out, so they pretended she was his new partner, and she worked charters with him when she could. The rest of the time, she managed the finances.

"Blaine is paying through the nose for everything," Gemma said, serenely and heard him chuckle. If Blaine kept anteing up, they might be in the black this year.

Gemma hadn't trusted the lawyer-hoping-to-turn-reality-host on sight, or even on second sight. Raymond Blaine's credit check was a bit concerning, so she'd insisted he pay each week of the charter upfront and in cash.

"You've got a better head for business than your old man," he said, a softer edge to his usual gruff.

"Dad loved this," Gemma said. Fish Bailey had been as much a character as Little Abner, but in a different way.

Fish, Gemma mentally paused to consider her father. Death was a funny thing. She'd learned more about him after he'd died than from living with him.

It was, she decided, a matter of perspective. She'd had none, or not much, as a daughter.

But he'd gradually become a person when she'd had to go through his things and unravel his life. He'd lived his life well below his mental abilities.

It was only after that she realized what an eccentric genius he'd been. His occasional trips to lecture or research a topic that interested him had been a part of the fabric of their life, so she'd viewed them as entirely normal.

It was probably the one trait that she could see that she shared with him: an insatiable curiosity for knowing things.

His quirky sense of humor had hidden this but the most discerning, or from people who'd known him a long time.

To the casual observer, Fish and Little Abner were like a comedy routine, with Little Abner as the straight man.

She knew Little Abner missed Fish as much as she did, but neither was good at expressing it.

They'd left Cocodrie early and were motoring up the bayou in the direction of Shark's Landing, though they were going to meet the courier—and the *special* guest—before they got that far North.

It was definitely odd, but odd was not that unusual in the charter business.

"He still asleep?" Gemma asked.

Little Abner shrugged. "As far as I can tell. She's sunbathing." His gaze flicked up, indicating she was above them on the fishing bridge.

"I hope she's dressed this time?" Apparently, Blaine's companion, Ashley, thought that up meant private.

"Mostly," Little Abner said, rolling his eyes.

He didn't approve of modern ways. And to be fair, he didn't have to. His boat, his rules.

"I suppose I should get breakfast going." Gemma sighed. It was hard to get excited about it when their guests were both clearly underwhelmed by her offerings. Not that she blamed them.

They'd made full disclosure about the food before confirming the booking. The galley was small, and Gemma was not a chef. Neither was Little Abner. All they'd promised was to not starve them.

Hence, the catering booking, she assumed. Blaine needed a special meal for his special guest.

Gemma didn't tell them she suffered along with them. She

liked good food, too. She just couldn't seem to produce it. It was like the opposite of a green thumb only with food. An un-flour thumb?

Little Abner's grin was sympathetic. He didn't care one way or the other. She assumed his taste buds had died a long time ago.

Little Abner could cook fish and they did when their charters caught some. But Blaine didn't even pretend to be fishing.

They'd been traversing the Gulf Coast in search of mythical creatures that Blaine didn't believe were mythical.

The lawyer wanted to become a reality show host.

He might do alright. He had a plummy voice that would sound authoritative. The slimy edges around his bluff and hearty might not show up on the small screen.

When Blaine wasn't talking about his show, he talked about the cheaters, scam artists, and swindlers he'd defended. His clear admiration for the more brilliant of these wasn't helped by his assertion he didn't defend murderers.

He had his standards, he declared.

Eye roll.

But now he wanted to try something new.

It wasn't that the path of sleazy lawyer to realty show host was such a huge leap. As near as she could tell, there were reality shows about almost everything. She knew modern courtrooms weren't like *Perry Mason*, but there was probably a lot of hand-wavium and histrionics to make it not unlike reality TV.

Blaine had, or so he believed, found a gap he could slide into. Hence the search for mythical creatures.

She was pretty sure his idea wasn't that unique, but she didn't have to buy it, just steer the boat and prepare lame meals.

They'd picked Blaine and Ashley up in Mobile, where he claimed to have caught footage of the Alabama's White Thang for his first sample show. They had then proceeded to Mississippi in search of some Pascagoula River Aliens. Now they were in Louisiana for his special meeting and to find the Rougarou.

She hadn't asked what this was, but he'd told her anyway. It was a man with a wolf or dog's head and a crap attitude. It sounded like a werewolf to her, but apparently the Rougarou was cursed, not bitten and it changed every night, not just on the full moon.

This could explain the crap attitude.

He'd already told her that the Rougarou was actually a Cajun accented version of the French *Loup-garou*—which was a werewolf.

She might have given a sigh. Blaine could have gone to France for his weird critter hunt, which also begged the question, how had the *Loup-Garou* gotten here? It's not like it could book passage.

She surrendered the helm to Little Abner and made her way down to the galley. She made a slight detour to check in with Ashley, who had a surprising penchant for Froot Loops for breakfast. She didn't eat them in front of Blaine, but that didn't seem to be a problem.

Raymond Blaine was not a morning person.

* * *

The local crime scene folks finished loading the corpse onto their air boat and handed over the evidence they'd collected.

They didn't show obvious relief—they were pros after all—but he had the sense of hands being washed and people moving on.

There was a rumble of engines and soon all that was left was them and the crime scene tape.

He eyed that, wondering how long it would last out here. And he hoped they wouldn't have to come back and find out.

Their driver had been patient, but he might have gunned the engine when they pulled away from the dock.

Dan was glad he was sitting down because his feet came off the boat's deck when their driver punched it.

The sun was low now, giving the swamp a different kind of creepy air. Moss draped cypress trees rose out of water that was varying shades of green fading to black in spots as the sun retreated.

He wouldn't call the air cooler, but it was less stifling than it had been coming in.

They were moving as fast as was safe, so the bugs were having trouble keeping up, thank goodness.

"Any idea where we can get something to eat?" Ruth asked the driver.

"If you don't mind a small detour into the bayou," he said, "my cousin has a place."

Ruth signaled approval for this and then settled back in her seat, her expression thoughtful. She was probably considering what they'd learned. That shouldn't take long. Would she mention the mutters of "Rougarou" from the two men who'd found the body.

You couldn't live in Louisiana and not know about the Rougarou. It was also not diplomatic to disbelieve the local legends. If your eyes were inclined to roll, keep it to yourself until you were alone was the advice even his dad had offered them at various times in their maturation process.

They'd all thought it was hilarious that Zach wouldn't say if he believed or not.

But in the face of the savagely scarred corpse? It was somewhat less hilarious. They shared their medical examiner with NCIS and he couldn't help but wonder if she'd be able to figure out what had caused the damage.

It was possible they might need some kind of expert. But what kind? There were those who specialized in shark bites, bear and tiger attacks, and even rats. If he did a search for a Rougarou expert, would he come up with anything useful? And did he really want that in his search history?

The other problem they had was that they knew who their victim had been, but not who he had become. No ID. No cellphone on or around the body. Hopefully, the forensics would find something on his clothing that would give them a place to start.

He thought he slipped into a slight doze because he jerked upright when the boat bumped against the dock.

He half expected Ruth to tweak him on the nap, but she just climbed out and stretched her kinked back.

He echoed the move. Their driver was already heading toward the seafood place, but Dan's gaze was caught by the sight of a sleek and well kept fifty-four-foot Hatteras docked just down from them.

He thought he heard soft music coming from its general direction.

"Nice," Ruth murmured. Her attention also caught by the boat. "*Reel Escape.* I know that name." She was quiet for a moment, then said. "Little Abner Abbot. Harry "the Fish" Bailey was his partner, but he died last year."

"Natural causes?"

Ruth flashed him a look that was mostly amused. "Yes. Heart attack, I think. Nothing suspicious, as I recall. Not that I was asked. I'm surprised to see it here. Abbot usually operates around the Florida coast."

Bailey must have been a civilian, Dan decided. "Eighties?" he asked, his gaze still on the boat. As Ruth had said, it was nice.

They resumed walking and Dan realized the small van parked not far from the boat had a familiar logo on its doors.

Blue Bayou Catering.

Crap. If Sarah was here, he was totally busted. Ruth didn't seem to notice.

"Yeah, they've been running charters since the late eighties," Ruth said. She half turned when she realized he'd stopped again. "Something wrong—"

She stopped in mid-sentence as a sleek and completely out-of-place limousine eased off the road and pulled to a stop near the *Reel Escape's* ramp, their side of the catering van.

Two bodyguards got out, covering the area while the driver came around to open the rear door for its occupant.

"Claude St. Cyr," Dan said, his tone both soft enough for Ruth's ears and shocked.

"You sure?"

"I'm sure." He couldn't mix the painfully narrow, pale and very cold face, of St. Cyr up with anyone else—unless it was the guy's mother. They were two peas out of the same corrupt pod.

They might have stared longer, but St. Cyr's gaze started to track their direction, so they both headed toward the seafood place.

Dan felt tension creep up his back. Sarah and St. Cyr? Cal would kill him if anything happened to Sarah. And if nothing happened? He was still busted.

Out of the corner of his eye, Dan saw St. Cyr board the *Reel Escape* and disappear from sight. Reluctantly, he held the door for Ruth, then followed her into the restaurant.

chapter two

Blaine's special guest was a major creeper. Gemma's skin crawled just looking at him. And she had to shake his hand—fish-cold and limp—and smile like she wasn't screaming inside.

There were people like that, people you knew were wrong inside, just by looking at them. If he hadn't arrived in a limo, she'd have cast him for a swamp zombie in Blaine's "reality" show.

He looked like a walking cadaver. Luckily, he didn't smell like one, but that said, his aftershave made her wish for a shower. It clung and cloyed.

His two bodyguards were total stereotypes, so much so they were almost boring. Almost. Because they were bodyguards of a creeper.

But weirdly, St. Cyr gave off worse vibes than the two—presumably—killers. It might be a cliche to think that these bodyguards were killers, but based on who they were guarding? It didn't feel like that much of a stretch.

The way St. Cyr looked at her made her glad she wore light-weight, sun-blocking pants and a shirt that covered her to the ankles and wrists. Her big sunhat shaded her face, and her Audrey Hepburn sunglasses hid her eyes. She was a huge Audrey fan.

She could make her gaze bland when called upon, but she was glad she didn't have to. She needed to be able to roll her eyes behind her glasses.

"You don't like the sun?" St. Cyr asked, his voice thin and cold.

"It doesn't like me," she replied. She'd practically grown up on the water, and no one would have guessed it from her tan—or rather her lack of one.

Her face was thin, freckled, and topped by a mop of pure carrot hair. In school, they'd called her Ghost Girl because she was that pale. Later this was reduced to GG for better conversational flow.

She knew that other girls—and even some guys—had body image issues. She didn't and she didn't know why. Some quirk in her makeup made her profoundly uninterested in what others thought about her.

She was interested in people, she liked watching them, so it was good she could usually fade into the background and observe.

Fading should have worked here. Ashley was gussied up like she was going to a garden show. Her hat had an even wider brim than Gemma's and her white dress was demurely sexy.

It was an interesting effect and it confirmed Gemma's impressions of her as much smarter than she liked men to realize.

She murmured a greeting and withdrew her hand from St. Cyr's grasp. The limp hold tightened for a second, but she tugged herself free and turned to Blaine.

"Fred has the food set out inside."

Ashley had only once protested about eating inside since she'd boarded. But after she accidentally ate a bug, she was fine with it.

Thankfully, it was Fred's job, as a representative of the catering company, to serve the special dinner.

"If you need me…." She trailed off, wishing her sunglasses gone for just a minute so her gaze could telegraph "don't need me."

"You won't be joining us?" St. Cyr's thin gray brows rose.

"No," Gemma said, unable to find a qualifier that wasn't more rude.

"She wouldn't be interested in our business," Blaine said, his tone more oily than usual.

Could St. Cyr be one of his legal clients? He didn't seem like the type to want a reality show about anything.

Good thing it wasn't her problem. She left without further comment and found Little Abner waiting with her bologna and raisin bread sandwich—Little Abner's speciality—all wrapped and waiting.

She might have given a slight sigh about the food she wasn't eating. It had smelled and looked really good when she was helping Fred set it out.

But maybe they wouldn't eat it all? A girl could hope.

"You could pop over to that seafood place," Gemma said. It would give her a chance to exchange her sandwich for something more palatable.

"I'm not leaving you alone with them," he said in his firmest tone, then his eyes began to twinkle. "I know how much you love my sandwiches, but you could pop over there if you want. You could use the break."

She grinned. "You sure?"

He picked up her sandwich. "Been eyeing it since I finished mine."

She grabbed her purse and left before he could change his mind.

* * *

The waitress was just setting down their plates when the woman walked in, letting the door swing closed behind her.

Dan was sure it wasn't an accident that Ruth had asked for a seat by a window, one that gave them a view of the *Reel Escape* outside and the entrance of this place.

So they'd seen her stroll down the ramp, a lightness to her step that was echoed in the swing of her shoulder strap purse.

There was almost no activity out there. It was too hot, but she would have stood out in any case.

For one thing, her clothes were at odds with the usual "scarcity is cooler" dress code. A glimpse of her pale face and hands gave her a good reason for covering up, but it seemed weird that someone that was sun adverse would be coming off a boat.

A random breeze tried to lift the wide brim of her hat and he'd thought he caught a glimpse of orange hair.

Once inside, the woman paused to remove sunglasses and hat, and looked around her. She smiled as the hostess approached and then followed as the hostess led her almost directly toward them.

It wasn't crowded. There was no reason for Dan to rise and gesture at the free chair next to Ruth, but it was as if his body followed a different imperative than his brain.

"Why don't you join us?"

He felt his cheeks warm and was thankful for the dim as she studied him for what felt like a long time. Her eyes widened and he thought they were gray, though it was hard to say. Her face was pale and freckled, but attractive for all that.

She glanced at Ruth who said, "please," in a tone that was downright welcoming for Ruth.

The woman's lips twitched and then she shrugged.

"Thank you." She set her hat on the empty table behind her and sank into the seat next to Ruth.

There was a bit more light coming in the window, giving him a chance to study her, even as he introduced himself and then Ruth, though minus the identifying rank of either of them.

"Gemma Bailey," she reciprocated.

Dan saw Ruth's lashes flicker at her last name.

Ruth half-turned, letting her eyebrows rise. "Fish Bailey a relative?"

Gemma's face relaxed a bit more. "You knew my father?"

"No." Ruth looked regretful. "Just heard his name around. Little Abner still aboard?" She half nodded toward the berthed boat.

"Of course," Gemma turned to give her order. "And I'll have a coke."

"What kind of coke?"

"Pepsi if you have it." She handed over her menu.

The server nodded and closed up her notebook.

This short interchange interrupted the natural flow that had been building. He tried to think of a way to get it going again.

Gemma gestured toward their plates. "Please, eat before it gets cold."

Dan bit into a shrimp and had to stop himself from groaning with pleasure. He was hungry and the shrimp was good. It wasn't a surprise to find good food almost anywhere in Louisiana, even the smallest wide spot in the road or along the bayou. When he'd chewed and swallowed, he gestured toward the boat with his fork.

"Nice."

Gemma's face lightened—which was kind of amazing, considering how pale she was beneath a tumbled mop of which was now clearly, decidedly carrot colored hair.

"She is."

"Limo is an odd sight," Ruth commented, her gaze not leaving her plate.

"Very." Gemma's tone was dry, but also uninformative. Her gaze shifted that way, just in time to see the driver, his cap pulled down as he leaned against the side, discouraging a small gaggle of kids from coming any closer. "Must be hot."

Tough duty even for a bad guy, Dan mentally agreed. He glanced at Gemma. She lifted her water for a sip, her gaze studying him over the rim.

The freckles that dotted her face gave her an urchin-like quality, but her gray gaze was level and intelligent. There was curiosity in them, but that was to be expected. What he didn't expect was the hint of wary.

She'd wonder why they'd invited her to join them. He wished he had an answer.

Their clothes provided no clues for her, though their jeans, shirts, and light jackets were a uniform of sorts—when combined with a badge. They'd stood out at their crime scene.

He had a feeling she was about to speak, when the waitress again interrupted, this time with Gemma's food and her soft drink.

Silence reigned because the food deserved it. When the plates had been pushed back, Gemma looked at Ruth, then at him.

"I was talking to one of the fishermen earlier. He said the Rougarou killed someone out in the swamp."

He and Ruth didn't exchange glances. They had more self-control than that.

"Well," Ruth qualified, "someone died out there."

Her words didn't confirm or deny their involvement, which was kind of a confirmation, he had to concede, when Gemma nodded slightly.

She appeared to consider something, then said with what felt like care, "Our charter is hoping for a Rougarou sighting."

Dan felt it appropriate to arch his brows, even as his brain tried to fit this revelation together with Claude St. Cyr.

"Lot of people have tried," Ruth said.

She didn't have to say they'd failed, other than some blurry photos now and again.

Gemma propped her elbows on the table. "When I was about sixteen, we were near the Everglades when they brought a body out. He was still alive but had been torn up pretty bad. Locals said it was the swamp ape."

Dan felt it appropriate to arch his brows higher and look briefly at Ruth.

"Seriously?" he asked.

"Swear it on my mama's grave."

"You saw him?" Ruth actually sounded shocked.

"Helped bandage him. It was an all-hands-on-deck situation because he was bleeding out."

"Tough situation," Dan said, a little curious about her rather matter-of-fact delivery.

"He survived," Gemma said, "but I heard he had issues."

Issues? Dan gave a little shake and tried not to smile.

"Not a surprise," Ruth said.

"No," Gemma agreed.

"You'd have had something to get over, too," Ruth said.

Gemma's pale red brows arched. "Me? Oh, right. Kids are kind of ghouls though." She was quiet for a moment. "The pattern of damage was consistent with an attack of some kind."

Her hands moved in the air as if remembering the slashes.

Was she playing them? Dan honestly couldn't tell. Locals did like to feed tales to gullible outsiders, but she was an outsider, or at least not an insider. Then he realized he wasn't sure, wondering what it was about her that made him sense she wasn't a local.

They needed more info on Gemma Bailey.

He had to quell an impulse to ask her to look at their body. Not only was it out of line, it wasn't a good idea when she'd just walked off a boat that St. Cyr was on.

Yeah, they definitely needed to know more about her.

chapter three

Gemma was thoughtful as she returned to the *Reel Escape* carrying four carryout bags.

She handed one to the limo driver as she went by, giving him smile in response to his surprised thanks.

She handed the other two to the bodyguards, and then carried the last one into Little Abner.

He'd be expecting it.

She took note of Ashley sitting out on the upper deck, as she went inside.

Little Abner was too interested in his food to notice her pensive mood. She debated whether to tell him about the unexpected invitation from Dan—Baker? She thought for a moment. Fossette, Ruth Fossette. They hadn't flashed badges, but she was pretty sure they were some kind law enforcement.

She couldn't put her finger on why exactly, because their clothes weren't crisp, which they wouldn't be if they'd been out in the swamp looking at a dead body. That was another good question. Why had she thought they'd know or were involved somehow? Wouldn't that be a local law enforcement problem?

For a minute, her lips twitching, she wondered if they were Men in Black, not wearing black, but here to investigate the

Rougarou. Yeah, she'd probably been out in the sun too long this trip.

But—there was no question in her mind that they gave off way different vibes than the creepy St. Cyr. And their interest in her—and the limo holding their guest—hadn't been casual.

"No problems?" she asked when Little Abner wiped his face and put the container to the side.

He shrugged. "Not that I know of."

She turned to stare out at the bayou trying to figure out what the creepy guy in the limo had to do with the hopeful reality show host slash sleazy lawyer.

She'd suspected the reality show was a cover story, though for what she couldn't imagine. But it was the other reason she'd made Blaine pay up front.

And if he was trying to involve them in something shady?

A sleazy lawyer and a creepy guy trying to get something shady going wasn't quite as far-fetched. St. Cyr could be a client maybe?

She didn't like that thought very much.

They had never required their clients to be Captain Americas, but they did have to be law-abiding.

It might be time to terminate their association. She'd insisted on a week-to-week deal, so they could if they needed to. If only she didn't know how bad Little Abner needed the money. Even her credit report hadn't put him off the charter. It wasn't like him to willingly spend this much time with a jerk like Blaine.

He could smell trouble on someone faster than she could say Rougarou.

Did that mean Blaine wasn't trouble? Or that Little Abner had decided to risk it? Was there a financial issue in his life he hadn't told her about? She had never, she realized now, run a credit or background check on Little Abner. She'd taken her dad's word that he was good people. And her own instincts confirmed that, but…

There was a lot she didn't know about her dad. He'd left

nothing but a few papers and his half of the *Reel Escape*. Had she hoped to find more about her mother? She still wasn't able to be honest with herself about that question. Most of the time she didn't have time to think about it. Besides, she was all grown up now.

She'd managed without a mother growing up, so why would she need one now? And she had Little Abner...

It had been a shock to see Little Abner after a winter apart. It felt like he'd gotten old overnight. Or over the last nine months. But he was the only family she had—using a broad definition of family of course.

She'd thought about doing one of those DNA tests from a genealogy site, but she kept getting stopped by, well, fear of what she'd find out or who'd she'd bring into her life. It wasn't as if she didn't have friends at work, friends who were almost family—

"I," Little Abner's voice broke into her thoughts. He glanced around and lowered his voice, "I don't like this. Maybe you should head back home."

"You could cancel the contract. I made sure it was week to week." She might have been fishing for a sense of where he stood.

He nodded. "Been thinking about that. But that's three days off." He met her gaze and it was familiar. "You could hitch a ride into New Orleans with Fred."

Her brows arched in surprise. "But if you cancel the contract..."

"I don't like that St. Cyr guy."

"I agree. But he's leaving." It hadn't been explicitly stated, but his limo was waiting for him. And they didn't have a berth for him. They were already full enough that she was sharing crew quarters with Little Abner.

She almost frowned. Was that why he wanted her to go? It was possible.

But they didn't really share that much, at least when they were sailing. One was on duty, one was off. It did get a little interesting while they were docked. How had they managed it when she was little, she wondered, realizing she'd had no awareness of those problems from back then. She'd slept in the bunk she occupied now, the top of course. But her dad had been in the lower. Or—she honestly didn't remember.

She opened her mouth to tell him about the two people she'd met when she noticed a shadow on the deck outside the hatch.

Was someone out there listening?

Little Abner arched his brows, so she pointed at the shadow.

Now Little Abner frowned, well, scowled was more like it. And, being the even-tempered man that he was—not—he strode quickly to the hatch and looked out.

"You need something?" he asked with pointed emphasis.

One of the bodyguards stepped into view.

"Just wanted to thank the lady for the lunch," he said, gruffly.

"You're welcome," Gemma said. When the man hesitated, she asked, "Was there something else?"

"Mr. St. Cyr wanted to say goodbye."

His sunglasses hid his expression, but the slight movement toward Little Abner, then back to her made her wonder if that request included them both.

But why would the creepy guy want to see either of them? Little Abner was, well, Little Abner and she? If there was an opposite of glamorous, that would be her. But there had been something there, she recalled from their meeting, just not something she remotely recognized. It was something that had raised the hair on her arms.

Little Abner nodded and walked out. The bodyguard waited for her, then followed them.

That wasn't creepy at all.

Both Blaine and St. Cyr were out on the deck and Ashley had joined them. Blaine and Ashley wore sunglasses as well, but there was a satisfied quirk to Blaine's mouth and an overall air of satisfaction. Ashley just looked bored.

Yeah, they needed to move on from this guy.

St. Cyr looked no different than he had when he arrived. It was as if he'd died and no one told him.

"Miss Bailey," the pale eyes were, if anything, colder than they'd been before. He nodded at her, then had a shorter nod for Little Abner. Perhaps he gave a signal of some kind, for the bodyguards stepped up and the small entourage left.

Gemma blinked behind her sunglasses.

And that wasn't weird—and creepy—either.

* * *

Ruth had given no sign of wanting to leave the restaurant, nor had she said anything since Gemma left.

They'd watched Gemma hand St. Cyr's driver one of the bags of food and carried the other three bags onto the boat. It was interesting, though not a surprise that St. Cry hadn't arranged for the man to eat.

He wondered what Ruth thought of it all, but he wasn't eager to open the topic since he still wasn't sure why he'd invited her to join them.

His feelings about Gemma Bailey were surprisingly conflicted. He dug around until he found the source and would have flinched if he were alone.

He liked her.

The intelligence, the directness of her brown gaze intrigued him. She wasn't beautiful, at least not by Hollywood standards. Or even his own, prior to today.

A thin, pale and freckled face? Carrot hair? A body equally as thin?

But the eyes had it. They pulled him in, so that he wanted to know more about her.

And he liked her.

None of them were good enough reasons to suspend his judgement. She was on a boat with a known mob figure.

And who was their charter that wanted to see a Rougarou? That smelled worse than the swamp.

He realized that Ruth was staring at him and arched his brows. He'd learned it was better to say as little as possible with Ruth. There was less chance of tripping over his own words and face-planting into embarrassed.

The pause was long and there might have been a hint of amused respect in Ruth's brown eyes.

"Interesting," Ruth finally said.

He nodded. He couldn't argue with that. It also wasn't much to work with.

"I have heard of St. Cyr, of course," Ruth said, at last. "Haven't had any dealings with him that I know of."

It was possible she'd helped to interdict some of his people, is what she meant.

Dan declined to mention that his sister-in-law was related to him. Ruth probably already knew that anyway.

"He's slippery, according to my brother, Frank." Frank was FBI, organized crime division.

"Wise guys usually are." She leaned back, blowing out a sigh. "We need to know more about what's going on there."

He didn't remind her they had a case. She knew. And he didn't disagree. He really wanted to know what was going on there, too.

He pulled out his cellphone and made the call to their small team back in the office.

"We should have something by the time we get back," he said.

"But should we go back?" Ruth murmured.

They were always prepared to stay if they had to. So much of what they did happened in unconventional spaces. And he wasn't sure where they'd stay, though. On the air boat? The thought made him shudder. They'd be eaten alive in an hour.

Just then St. Cyr and his bodyguards appeared at the top of the ramp and all three climbed quickly back in the limo. It turned and started back the way it had come.

"I could try Frank, see if he knows anything," Dan offered,

without a lot of enthusiasm. His brother would want to know why he was asking when he was supposed to be out in the Gulf rescuing people.

Ruth shook her head. "Wouldn't even know what question to ask." A slight, wicked glint appeared in her eyes. "We do have our body we're investigating. We should probably question everyone here on the dock. For local information."

Dan grinned. At the moment, the only boat moored to the dock was the *Reel Escape.*

* * *

It was kind of funny how no one moved after St. Cyr's departure. The sound of their retreating steps briefly drowned out the drone of insects. The boat rocked a bit as they disembarked and after a short wait, the limo's engine fired, followed by the crunch of tires as it left.

Gemma wanted to finish her talk with Little Abner, but alone. It was weird how they still weren't moving. And then, amazingly, they heard someone call out.

"Ahoy, *Reel Escape,* permission to come aboard?"

Gemma exchanged a startled look with Little Abner and they both crossed over to where they could see the dock.

It was her lunch companions, Ruth and Dan.

He looked even better with the sun glinting off his brown hair, finding interesting highlights in the strands. He had a strong, sturdy build and a cleanly formed, good-guy face.

His clothes were definitely rumpled but he still somehow managed to give off a crisp vibe. Ex-military, perhaps?

Ruth was a tougher nut to parse, though Gemma still thought she had to be law enforcement. She was lean and tough, both in the way she held herself and the set of her mouth.

They were kind of an odd pair. They fit—but didn't.

Maybe it was their sense of shared purpose?

Just what was that purpose?

"I met them at lunch," Gemma said before Little Abner could speak.

"Oh?" He hesitated, then lifted a hand, signaling they could board. She could tell he wished they could talk, too, as they turned to walk down and meet these unexpected guests.

As Gemma looked back, she noted that Blaine shared an uneasy look with Ashley.

What were those two up to?

Was it going to hose them, too? She sure didn't want the *Reel Escape* to get impounded over them. Local law enforcement had the power to impound and ask questions later.

She and Little Abner reached dockside and found the two waiting there, both looking keenly around.

"Nice," Ruth said. Her attention turned to Little Abner, retaining keen in her gaze and adding in a lot of assessing.

Little Abner was unperturbed, but Gemma noted he did straighten his shoulders a bit and may have even sucked in his stomach.

Gemma glanced between them one more time and felt her brows try to hitch a little. She turned her attention to Dan to distract herself. His lips twitched and then firmed. She added "has a sense of humor" to his positives, but didn't kid herself that there wasn't a negative or two incoming.

She saw Dan's gaze flick up and realized Blaine and Ashely must be up there looking down on them.

"Afternoon," Dan said pleasantly.

"Afternoon," Blaine said in his hale-and-hearty-well-met-tone, with a little of I-have-nothing-to-hide thrown in there.

So he wasn't happy, and she was ninety-nine percent sure he had something to hide.

Normally, Gemma wouldn't have cared, but there were too many signs of dodgy about Blaine. Ashley? She kept forgetting her bimbo role too often for Gemma to feel inclined to underestimate her.

Ruth pulled out a folder and showed a badge. She and Little Abner leaned in to study it.

Her first thought was, crap. The Coastguard? They could totally impound their boat. She didn't think they could keep it, but it would take time to get it back. This would totally hose Little Abner's finances—at least the ones she knew about. It would probably hose the stuff she didn't know, too.

She tried to quell panic and squinted at the rest of it. CGIS? She looked up, letting her face ask the question.

"Coast Guard Investigative Service," Dan said, holding up his badge, too.

Daniel Baker. His photo didn't do him justice. How was that even possible? Her official photos ranged from horrible to unrecognizable.

"I've never heard of it," Gemma admitted.

"Is there a problem?" Little Abner's tone was pitch perfect helpful and curious.

Did that mean he had heard of CGIS?

"We're a small team," Dan admitted, with an easy grin.

"Gemma mentioned there are some rumors circulating about the body found in the swamp," Ruth said, snapping the ID closed. "We were wondering if we could ask you some questions?"

Gemma noted that, while Ruth mentioned the body, she didn't limit the range of her questions to it.

Ruth glanced up. "All of you?"

"Of course," Little Abner said.

Gemma had known Little Abner for as long as she'd been alive, but she totally didn't know what the almost flourishing gesture indicated. It was almost courtly.

Ruth knew her way around boats, obviously, and had no trouble finding her way to the upper deck where Blaine and Ashley had seated themselves in "we have nothing to hide" poses.

Gemma gave an internal wince. Had she ever had so many

internal quotes in her thoughts? They definitely needed to get both Blaine and Ashley offloaded. She started to calculate when that might be possible as she crossed over and leaned against the rail.

She lifted her chin, hoping for a bit of a breeze, but the air was damp and leaden.

"They are wondering if you heard anything about the body that was discovered…" Little Abner trailed off and raised an interrogatory brow.

"It was discovered last night," Ruth said, opening a notebook as if to remind herself of the details.

"They're saying it was the Rougarou," Gemma put in, well aware of the effect it would have on Blaine—if he really was hoping for a sighting.

Blaine straightened with a jerk, his gaze traveling around the group. "A Rougarou? Where?"

Dan's lips twitched. "Hunting camp in the swamp south of Chauvin." He stepped forward, a hand out, forcing Blaine to scramble to his feet to clasp it. "Daniel Baker, CGIS."

"Raymond Blaine," Blaine said, shaking Dan's hand, then turning to gesture toward Ashley. "My associate, Ashley Hammond."

Ashley made a fluttery move with her hand but didn't move from her reclining position. She still wore her garden party clothes, though she had removed the wide-brimmed hat and secured a drink that looked freshly chilled.

"They think it was the Rougarou?" Blaine said now, his expression eager.

What was he really interested in out there? Gemma wondered. He hadn't shown them any of his so-called footage of the other creatures, though he had extolled it as epic more than once.

"That's what some of them are saying," Ruth said, as if this were normal.

Maybe it was around here.

"I need to get out there," Blaine said, striding from one rail to the other and then turning back to them.

Gemma saw Ruth and Dan exchange looks that were curiously devoid of expression indicators.

"What are you doing here, Mr. Blaine?" Ruth asked, her intent expression at odds with her easy tone.

Blaine tried to look modest. Failed. Gemma didn't award him points for trying. He'd meant to fail.

"I'm working on a reality show."

"A *reality* show?" The faint lift of Dan's brows was perfect. "About the Rougarou?"

Gemma had to bite back a chuckle.

"Not just the Rougarou!" Blaine flung his hands out. "We've stopped at various places on the way here to film other so-called mythical beasts. I hope to do a weekly episode on the beastly legends of each state. If the show is successful, then I'll branch out to other countries."

"And Claude St. Cyr?" Dan dropped the question as if it wasn't the one they'd come to ask, Gemma decided. "What's his role in this show?"

Blaine's expression faltered for a second, but he recovered quickly. "He's interested in investing in the show."

Neither Ruth, nor Dan said anything. They just stared at Blaine as if waiting for more.

It was obvious Blaine didn't have more because he hadn't seen this coming.

"Who is St. Cyr?" Little Abner asked. "I don't keep up on television or movies."

"It wouldn't help if you had," Ruth said dryly.

"St. Cyr," Dan came in as if on cue, "is a known leader of a crime syndicate in New Orleans."

Blaine started artistically back, with the right amount of alarm on his face. "I had no idea!"

Gemma had a feeling Ashley was rolling her eyes behind her sunglasses.

"I'm not from around here," Blaine added.

"I didn't think you were," Ruth said.

How did she keep her tone so dry in the humidity, Gemma wondered, appreciatively.

"I can't tell you how much I appreciate the warning. I will definitely have to reassess my involvement with the man." He didn't do a bad job at sounding sincere. It was probably how he'd got so many of his scummy clients off the legal hook.

"You didn't do a background check on him before the meeting?" Dan was keeping his contributions casual.

Gemma couldn't call them good cop or bad cop, but they were definitely clever, like a comedy team without the funny parts.

"It was a spur of the moment meeting," Blaine said after a brief hesitation, that wasn't suspicious at all.

Spur of the moment? Gemma would have snorted. She was sure he could have arranged the catered meal at the last minute…not.

Which reminded her that she needed to see if Fred needed anything before he pushed off. And if there were any leftovers on hand. Yes, she'd had lunch, but man, that had smelled good.

"Have you been in television long?" Ruth asked.

"Me? I'm not in television yet. I'm hoping for a career change with this venture."

"Interesting," Ruth said.

"And what career are you changing from?" Dan asked.

Blaine swallowed a bit dryly, Gemma thought.

"Lawyer."

"Funny how many lawyers seem to want to change careers," Dan said. "My little sister just started with a firm in New Orleans. She's hoping to be a prosecutor someday though."

Blaine managed to look even less thrilled. "I'm, I was, a defense lawyer, for the most part. But that's behind me now."

He wasn't quite so braggy about his brilliant saves of swindlers and other scummy types today, she noted.

Gemma straightened. "If you'll excuse me, I need to go check on Fred."

She didn't wait for permission, just left, though not without a pang. Dan was the best scenery she'd had since they'd headed up this bayou.

* * *

Dan wished he could think of a reason to go after Gemma. Something about her drew him in a way he couldn't quite figure out, but it wasn't just that. He'd like to have gotten her take on this setup if only he thought she'd tell him.

"Fred?" he asked. At least Gemma hadn't mentioned Sarah.

"From the caterer," Abner Abbot explained.

Dan noted Blaine's discomfort at this information. Not a surprise, since it didn't jive with his last-minute meeting explanation. Relief warred with wary. Clearly Sarah wasn't here.

"So how do you go about filming the Rougarou?" Ruth asked, shifting against the railing in a way that signaled a kind of permanence.

Blaine relaxed, an indication he liked this question. "I have several portable cameras, those Get Pro ones, three for me and one for my guide."

That he didn't know Go-Pro was not a good sign. But he probably didn't have to know what they were called to use one. Dan exchanged a glance with Ruth. "Guide?"

"A local. Pascal Ledet." Ashley Hammond contributed this in a bored tone.

"You're not going with them?" Dan asked. What was her role in all of this? Other than the obvious.

"I don't do swamps." She lowered her glasses and studied him for a long moment. "I edit the film for him when he gets back."

Dan was aware he'd done a swamp today and he looked it. Now it felt like he smelled it, too.

"You could take me out to lunch while he's gone," she said, her tone suddenly too sultry for the hot day.

"Agent Baker is on duty," Ruth said.

"Dinner?"

Now he saw a hint of mischief in her eyes. It was more attractive than the bored one, but she wasn't his type. He hesitated at that thought. Since when? Cool blondes usually were his type. Maybe it was the lingering aura of St. Cyr. It sure wasn't the skinny red head talking to Fred in the galley.

"We'll be working until we sort out our dead body," Dan said.

Unfazed, she shrugged. "Pity."

"You could head up to New Orleans," Blaine suggested.

She'd lifted her sunglasses back in place, so Dan couldn't tell what she thought of that idea.

"And how would I get there, darling Raymond?"

Blaine glanced around, his gaze studying the nearly empty dock. "The catering truck?"

"I'm almost that desperate."

Dan felt the air change and looked around, his attention settling on some low, fast moving clouds.

"Gonna rain," he said.

Abner Abbot nodded agreement. "Let's move inside. Gully washer for sure."

He was quickly proved right. The light darkened, thunder crashed, following quickly were lightning and the heavy rain that blurred the view through the windows. The one hundred percent humidity got impossibly worse, too.

It felt closer inside, as if everyone were up in each other's grill. Ashely Hammond drifted over to one of the windows, leaned against it, her attention outward even though she couldn't see much through the blurry glass.

Abner Abbot stood with his feet planted, his powerful arms crossed, blocking the sliding doors to the deck, looking almost stereotypically grumpy.

Blaine had edged as far from he and Ruth as the space allowed and now stood, slouching with his hands shoved in his pockets.

The rain rattled against every part of the boat, discouraging the conversation that no one appeared to want to have anyway.

Ruth, as was her usual, appeared unperturbed by the storm or the lack of conversation. But Dan was pretty sure her gaze never left Blaine.

Gradually the rain began to taper off and Abbot seemed to come to himself.

"Was there anything else I can help you with?" he asked. In contrast to his face, his tone was friendly. Interesting that he directed the question to Ruth.

"That's all for now," she said, "though…how long will you be here or in the area?"

Abbot looked at Blaine. "We're heading through the canal to Lake Boudreaux as soon as Fred takes off. We're meeting the guide there."

Ruth glanced at her watch. "Bit late.

"We plan to go in at dusk," Blaine said. Maybe something in their expressions or body language got him to add, "It won't be my first time in the swamp at night. I've filmed the Swamp Skunk, the White Thang, and the Pascagoula River Aliens."

All Dan could manage was a blink.

"And your guide knows where to wait for the Rougarou?" Ruth asked.

"Well, in the general area," Blaine said. "Ledet has a hunting camp with a hide. We thought we'd set up there, though as a local I'm sure he knows where your incident occurred."

"I'm sure he does," Dan said.

"I hope you'll have plenty of bug repellant," Ruth said.

Blaine gave a laugh that sounded forced. "We'll be fully kitted out."

Dan didn't ask if they'd be armed. He didn't know a Cajun who wasn't. He glanced at Ruth and got the signal to go.

"Thanks for your help," he said, Ruth chiming in with her official sounding thanks.

Abbot went with them to dockside. To Dan's surprise, he stepped ashore with them.

"If I can help, don't hesitate," he said, pulling out a grimy business card and handing it to Ruth.

She glanced down at it, then met his gaze and gave him what Dan would call a careful smile.

She wasn't sure what to make of the old guy, Dan decided. Not that this was much of a surprise. He wasn't sure what to make of him—or Gemma—either.

As if on cue, she appeared up on the deck. He tried to think what she reminded him of, standing there with her wide brimmed hat shielding her face from the sun. Her dark glasses were huge and white-rimmed and her sun-blocking pants and shirt drifted lightly around her, as if they managed to find a phantom breeze off the canal.

But even more than wondering who she reminded him of, he wondered why he liked the look of her gamin figure up there. The air felt less hot and lighter somehow.

"Leaving already?" she asked.

"Duty calls," he said.

"It does like to do that," she agreed. "Perhaps I'll see you around."

Dan glanced around and grinned. "You'll certainly see me coming."

She laughed and the sound of it made his nerve endings quiver weirdly.

Who was she?

He and Ruth headed back toward the restaurant to hook up with their airboat driver. If Ruth didn't want to leave, then they'd most likely head to Duval and the Coast Guard station there. He hoped they had a corner for them somewhere.

He couldn't help but glance back. That's when it hit him.

She reminded him of Audrey Hepburn. He wasn't sure what movie, because he didn't think he'd watched one all the way through. It was weird, though because she didn't look at all like her. Red hair and freckles instead of white skin and dark hair.

No, it was something much more subtle. Was it weird to wish one of his sisters were here to figure it out for him? Even while being profoundly grateful none of them were within one hundred miles?

"Do you know who she reminds me of?" Ruth said, stopping to look back with him.

Gemma had started to move along the deck and disappeared from sight.

"Who," he asked.

"Audrey Hepburn. How weird is that?"

"Totally weird," he said. "She looks nothing like her."

"I know." Ruth shook her head and turning, went inside.

After a last look back, Dan followed her.

chapter four

Gemma pushed back her laptop with a sigh and reached for her soft drink. It was nicely cold in its refrigerated holder, but the chill of it faded about halfway down her throat, leaving her feeling somehow hotter.

Another storm had passed through, thickening the air with evaporating water. It felt like every part of her body was damp and sticky.

At least it was just her and Little Abner. Ashley had taken the ride with Fred, much to his delight. And Blaine and Ledet had pushed off at dusk yesterday.

Little Abner had moored them a safe distance offshore from where the two men had gone into the swamp. They'd agreed that as soon as he got back, they'd talk to him about ending their contract. At least Little Abner had seemed as relieved as she was, easing some of her fears.

That hadn't stopped her from launching a quick background check on him, Dan, and Ruth. Dan and Ruth were pretty much open books, too.

Dan and Ruth were what they said they were. A picture popped up of him with his brother. She'd sometimes wondered what it would be like to have a sister or brother.

Whatever Little Abner was worried about, it wasn't obvious in his public record. She was surprised to find he'd been born in Montana. He was such a 'man of the sea' type. He even had the accent.

So now she felt guilty about sneaking a look into Little Abner's life—and surprised parts of it hadn't made it into his stories. It felt a bit like she'd peeked into his closet or at least a place she hadn't been invited into.

She reached for the command to close out the connection but before she could, she got pinged by her boss. That's what she got for using her work's for the searches. She wouldn't get in trouble for using the access for personal reasons. She was too valuable to Seth, but she didn't like getting caught.

Why aren't you enjoying your vacation, Shadow?

Usually her time on the *Reel Escape* was decompression time and Seth was fine with it because she came back ready to dive back into work.

Why do you think I'm not?

Their interactions often resembled a tennis match. He'd serve and she'd lob it back at him. She wasn't surprised when he didn't answer right away. It must be tough for him to know and pretend not to know.

You don't usually work while you're there.

Not bad. And it was true. She liked to leave it all back there and just be Gemma. Was he worried she wasn't coming back? Her last meeting with Seth had been unsettling and she still wasn't sure why.

Seth was probably the single other certainty in her life, after Little Abner. He did what he did, and she did what she did with no drama. But had there been actual drama in their last meeting? She did have a low drama threshold for her work life. She wasn't wild about it in her private life, but accepted it as the cost of being alive.

Maybe something or someone outside of work was stirring his pot, though it was totally not like him to bring any of that into the workspace.

Typically Seth was cooler than St. Cyr—though not as creepy. But he didn't do emotion. She kept going over and over the scene in her mind, trying to figure out what had been different, what had unsettled her. And trying to figure out why she was reluctant to head back when Little Abner clearly wanted her to go.

Seth was a little bit Alan Rickman and a little bit Cary Grant, though without an accent of any kind. He could have hailed from anywhere. Carefully neat dark hair loomed over a thin, clever face, and piercing almost-black eyes. He was tall and elegant, and had a cool charm that went over well with the clients he deigned to meet with personally, which wasn't often. He had "someone" for that most of the time.

His someone was Valka Bland. Every time Gemma heard it or thought it, her brain twitched. It was as if her parents had tried to find a name totally opposite of Bland.

Not only were her names extreme opposites, but Valka was wrong for her age. Ms. Bland was well into her sixties, possibly even her seventies. Her hair was sternly gray, and her eyes had a yellow cast to them, as if she wore contact lens. Or she was a wolf at night. That felt entirely possible.

Gemma was sure she'd had plastic surgery done at some point. Her nose was too perfect, and her chin was sharp enough to wound or even kill.

Her posture was perfect and her high fashion black apparel gave off a mixed message, at least in Gemma's opinion.

To their clients, she was a firm, but sympathetic grandma, or maybe the doyenne of a creepy orphanage? She could never decide.

To the employees like Gemma, she was mostly ruthless personal assistant, devoted to Seth's interests.

From Gemma's perspective, Valka sorted the clients into the right bucket (Gemma being one of the buckets). If Valka did anything else, Gemma wasn't in that information loop.

Valka always implied she was more and at times Gemma had wondered if she was Seth's mother.

When Valka was around, Gemma kept expecting the proverbial—or actual—knife in the back. The only time she didn't feel it was when she was heading out on vacation.

It wasn't exactly pleasure Valka exuded at that time. Gemma wasn't sure she could. But Gemma leaving seemed to make Valka as happy as Valka could be—which wasn't much.

Gemma didn't know why Valka didn't like her. She had no aspirations to take her place. She'd never been able to keep the "Morticia" look in place for more than a minute before dissolving into giggles.

She'd finally decided that some women couldn't help defending their turf, even when it wasn't under attack.

If Seth noticed or thought anything about it, he never said or showed any awareness. Seth's detachment was just shy of inhuman.

Gemma considered this and realized it wouldn't have surprised her to find out he was a vampire. And she had no problem seeing Valka as his Renfield.

She was aware of the irony of the two principal men in her life behaving in ways that weren't typical. She didn't like it, but there wasn't much she would do about it.

She hesitated, then typed: *I'm not working.*

Let him make what he would of that. If he fired her, she'd go to work for some park service somewhere, which was what she'd actually planned to do with her life.

"It's hot," Little Abner stated the obvious from his seat across the deck from her.

She closed her laptop without waiting to see Seth's response. "I think it passed hot a long time ago."

Little Abner chuckled. "Funny how it's hot all along the Gulf coast, but each place has its own special brand of hot."

Now it was her turn to chuckle. "I hadn't thought of that, but you're right."

Of course, out here on the water, the humidity was higher, but the chances of catching a breeze were better. In the distance she could see boats bobbing here and there. Private and commercial fishing boats, she knew, and a few smaller cargo craft.

Despite the layer of moisture on her skin, she leaned back with a sigh. She needed to get back to enjoying the moment.

Little Abner shifted in his seat, the look on his face reminding her of the way he'd looked at Ruth. She opened her mouth to ask and closed it again. She'd been snooping too much in his life already.

"This is nice," she said instead. "I wish Blaine weren't coming back."

Little Abner grunted what was probably agreement. He liked sharing his love of the ocean and fishing with his charters, but he was always relieved when they left and he got his boat to himself again.

She glanced up and noticed the angle of the sun. She looked at her watch and frowned.

"Blaine and Ledet should be back by now, shouldn't they?" she asked.

"They aren't overdue yet," Little Abner said, but he rose to peer out toward the small bayou the two had used to enter the swamp.

"Five minutes to overdue and they expected to be back before noon."

She still couldn't believe Blaine had been willing to spend the night in the swamp. He hadn't wanted to give them an overdue time until she pointed out that if they did get stranded, they would be glad to know that at some point someone would come looking for them.

Little Abner had the Terrebonne Sheriff's office on speed dial. It was the first thing he'd done when Ledet's pirogue had disappeared into what sunset the swamp hadn't swallowed up. *Pee-row.* An interesting word for an interesting boat.

She'd looked it up when Ledet had first been mentioned. A pirogue—*pee-row*—was a shallow wooden boat, used in the swamps because it could skim across shallow water.

When she'd asked why not an airboat, Blaine had pointed out the need for a quiet approach. That made as much sense as was possible when dealing with a mythical creature.

She kept circling back to wondering what was really going on there.

"I'll give them a little more time," Little Abner said, but he didn't return to his seat.

"Do you think he's really looking for the Rougarou?" She rose and joined him at the rail.

"I've seen stranger things," Little Abner said, which wasn't exactly an answer.

She thought about pressing the issue, but it was hot and did she really want to know? As she knew all too well, when you found out things, you had to do something about them. That's why she tried to stay in her lane—which was wide enough to give her plenty to deal with.

She turned, leaning against the rail, and looked at Little Abner. His reaction to that Coast Guard agent sent her thoughts in a new direction. If he was interested in Ruth—as weird as that felt to her—maybe he wanted her to leave for a more personal reason? She almost shuddered at the thought of being a third wheel in that situation.

"Once we offload Blaine, do you want me to find something else to do? Something not on board?"

He glanced at her. "You think I'm kicking you off?"

"Nudging is the word I'd use. It's okay. It might take me a while to take a hint, but I get there eventually."

Little Abner didn't speak or look at her, so she turned so that they stood shoulder to shoulder.

"We're the closest we each have to family. If we can't be honest with each other without getting mad about it…"

He looked at her then and started to speak, but a sound cut across his words. They both turned and saw a boat that looked to be on course toward them.

It angled its approach and slowed, so it could pull in alongside them, giving them a good look at the Coast Guard logo on the side. And the two passengers. Dan and Ruth.

She probably ought to quit calling them by their first names. They were agents, not new acquaintances.

They both went down to the aft side ladder. Little Abner caught the rope one of the crew tossed him and secured it. Ruth and Dan scrambled up the ladder. No one followed them. Not an official boarding party then.

She realized she was uneasy, but not enough. She hadn't thought she'd see him—them again. She might have even hoped a little that she would. She'd like him—them—at their impromptu lunch.

The sun was lowering, but still hot, so they made their way to the air-conditioned saloon on the flybridge. Other than minimal greetings, no one spoke.

Dan looked even better today. In the closer confines of the salon, he smelled good. Something rugged and spicy. And his hair had been artfully stirred up by the ride. Dang, he was cute, but he also had a lethal—yet good guy—competence that wasn't surprising given his career choice.

Why did she have to resist the urge to shift from one foot to the other, not to mention wanting to twisted some strands of her hair around a finger?

Her hair was twisted up to keep it off her neck. What strands had escaped were not really suitable for twisting. She tried one of the thicker chunks and had to hide a wince. No, not suitable for that.

What was her problem?

She pulled off her sunglasses and tossed them onto a counter, turning back to their visitors. Her gaze intersected Dan's—no, Agent Baker. The look in his eyes wasn't too agenty. It almost seemed like something warm flared in their depths, before a professional mask replaced the friendly expression on his face.

She'd had a lot of practice controlling her expression, so the electric shock didn't show, though she felt it pass through her body.

Oh. So that's what it was.

She read romances to relax. She knew how things worked. And she knew how it mostly didn't work in her life.

She tried to remember the last time she'd felt any kind of attraction for a guy. There'd been a few over the years, but none of them had looked at her like that. She had a mirror. She knew why and didn't blame them. Even the ones that sparked her interest—it faded pretty fast. Usually the fade started soon after they started talking about themselves.

It was part of her job to be underestimated, so it was never a surprise when they got condescending. But sometimes it was a disappointment.

She'd mostly found men as uninteresting as they found her. The ones who feigned interest did it because of what—and who she knew—not who she was. She gave a slight sigh because she might wish it would be different this time, that maybe her liking would intersect with his.

She didn't get her hopes up. It's not like Dan—Agent Baker—was encouraging her in anyway.

So how should she handle this? This was new territory for her. Then she almost laughed. Handle what? There wasn't anything to handle here. Or if there was, time and distance would end it, especially if Little Abner did boot her so he could court the Coastie.

She dragged her attention off Dan and directed it to Little Abner and Ruth. They weren't any closer than she and Dan, but there was definitely something radiating from Little Abner. She could see no sign that Ruth was radiating back—or that she knew she was being radiated at.

She had to look away, which made her gaze connect with Dan's. He looked amused, too. They both looked away at the same time. She knew she was afraid she'd grin, so he might be, too.

Ruth glanced casually around. "Blaine not back yet?"

"He should have been," Little Abner said. "We were just debating whether to call search and rescue."

Gemma didn't react to this reframing of their conversation, but she couldn't look at Little Abner. A giggle would be so not appropriate at the moment.

Ruth's well marked brows arched. "How far overdue is he?"

"He told us he'd be back around noon, but insisted we not raise the alarm until about now," Gemma said. "Did you need to see him urgently?"

"We had some more questions for all of you, and a photo of our victim," Ruth said.

Gemma felt an unnatural moment of hope that the photo would be post-Rougarou, then realized how unlikely that was.

"You think Blaine knew him?" Little Abner sounded surprised. "We only arrived in the area a couple of days ago."

"We're wondering if our victim was in Cocodrie." Dan said easily. "We haven't been able to find any indication he came down from Chauvin or parts north."

It sounded so funny to think of Chauvin or any of Louisiana as north, but they were really far south.

Dan pulled two rectangles out of his jacket pocket and handed them to her.

"One is from his Coast Guard ID and the other has been aged to show what he probably looked like now."

Gemma stifled an irreverent thought about the aged photo being post-Rougarou encounter. Sometimes she was embarrassed by herself. At least her time working for Seth had taught her not to say what she was thinking.

She took the photographs, holding both photos so she could study them.

Little Abner moved closer to look at it, too. His arm touched hers, which is why she felt the slight stiffening. Did he know this guy? The official looking photo looked old, like last century old. The color was grainy, older tech color film.

The man had the look and bearing to go with the uniform. He

was probably in his mid-thirties. She turned the photo over but there was no date on it and the paper felt newer. It had probably been printed out so they could show it around.

Little Abner took it from her.

"He looks a bit like someone I used to know, a long time ago," Little Abner said. "He'd be old now if he were still alive…" He broke off.

Of course he wasn't still alive. He'd been found dead in the swamp.

Little Abner met their gazes with the expression he used to deflect annoying passengers. "Do I need to try to remember his name?"

Gemma's lips might have twitched.

"Henry Perkins," Ruth said. "That's from his official Coast Guard ID."

Was there a hint of amusement in her voice? If it was there, it was very subtle.

Little Abner stood frowning down at the photo. "There's something I feel like I should remember…" He shook his head. "It's been a long time."

"Late eighties," Dan said. "A private plane went missing. Possible crash. No one was ever found."

Little Abner rubbed his face. "Getting a vague memory."

Was it her imagination that his hand trembled slightly.

"The pilot was a Chester Milken and there was a female passenger," Ruth said.

Little Abner looked at her. The puzzled part might be real.

"How could this Perkins be your victim if he disappeared back then?"

Gemma did some mental math and came up with a figure that felt unsettling. This Perkins and Little Abner would have been close to the same age in the late eighties.

"It's a problem," Dan admitted. "Apparently, he was late for his own death."

Gemma bit her lips and half turned away until she got the

urge to laugh under control. They were talking about a dead guy. Now was not the time to lose control of her sometimes inappropriate sense of humor—even if it would have been good distraction for her thoughts and her math.

"The crash site was never found," Ruth said, "though authorities and civilians looked for it off and on over the years."

Gemma could tell Little Abner's wheels were turning. Actually, her own wheels were turning. Could Blaine be looking for that plane? But…it didn't make sense unless there had been something valuable on that plane. She wanted to shake her thoughts out and start over. She was *not* going to conjure a treasure hunt out of the humid air. But…

A treasure hunt made more sense than looking for a Rougarou or the other creatures Blaine had supposedly filmed.

Were the other stops a smokescreen? Or research? As she well knew, there was new technology available for finding missing people—especially if they were missing because they didn't want to be found.

If Perkins walked away, then so would anything valuable, surely?

"It's something of a legend," Dan added. "Conspiracy theorists have gotten involved."

"The Rougarou?" Gemma asked, "or alien abduction?"

"Both." Dan grinned.

"And some rumors of lost treasure," Ruth said, "but you have to dig a little deeper for those theories to appear."

Gemma found she didn't mind being a conspiracy theorist that much. It might have made her want to smile.

But, conspiracy theories aside, who would walk away alive from a crash? Or a planned landing? It could be either. Who would do that, and not take their treasure with them?

She turned and gazed in the direction Blaine and Ledet had gone.

If it had been a crash, and it had happened around here…it could make the walking away more challenging.

"Do they say what the treasure is or was?" Gemma asked, still gazing out over the water towards the swamp.

"No," Dan said, coming over to stand next to her, "but apparently it is guarded by the Rougarou."

"He's a busy monster," Gemma murmured.

She looked down at the photos she still held. Had she seen him during their short stop in Cocodrie? If she had, something would ping inside her head. It might take time, but she'd remember. It was one of the reasons she was so good at her job.

She didn't have an eidetic memory, but hers was close. She ran her thoughts back to Cocodrie, replaying their actions and trying to "see" the people around them.

"Did you see Blaine meet with anyone there?" Ruth asked, somewhat distantly

"I didn't see him," she finally said, certainty in her voice, "and I didn't see Blaine meet with anyone."

Little Abner took longer to answer. Was he really trying to remember or wondering if he should admit he'd seen him?

"I don't think so," Little Abner finally said. "What name was he using?"

Dan and Ruth exchanged looks. "We're still trying to find that out. He didn't have ID on his body."

Facial recognition technology might help, but it took time. And it also depended on how hard Perkins had tried to hide.

"Was your arrival to schedule?" Dan asked.

Little Abner shrugged. "More or less. We always try to allow some give if we have to go around a storm and Blaine took longer ashore looking for his river aliens than he'd planned."

Out of habit, her brain was doing its slow spin. *Not your problem. Not your job.* She was on vacation, she reminded herself. And if she tried, they'd think she was one of those amateur detectives or something and be annoyed. She'd read this scenario and seen it in movies and TV. Nope. No way.

That didn't stop her from wishing she could see the crime scene photos.

"Did Blaine leave any belongings behind?" Ruth glanced around. "And Miss Hammond? Did she go with him?"

Gemma shook her head. "Ashley hitched a ride with Fred, the catering guy. She took everything of hers with her."

Gemma had given the room a quick go over and changed the sheets so she and Little Abner could quit sharing the crew quarters. She'd have to clean it again, if Ashley came back but it was worth it to get a break from Little Abner's snoring.

"And Blaine?" Dan asked.

Agent Baker.

"I don't think so," Gemma said. She hadn't looked. It was not her policy to snoop through the guest quarters even if she had felt the urge. She'd hinted she'd like to see his footage and been blandly ignored. Now she wondered if it even existed.

"Do you mind if we look?" Ruth asked.

And if they did mind? They were Coast Guard. They could look where they wanted. Gemma made a gesture with her hand.

"I'll show you," Little Abner said to Gemma's surprise.

Ruth left with him and Dan—Agent Baker—stayed behind. Well, Blaine's stateroom was pretty small, and it shouldn't take them long to see if he'd left anything.

The silence wasn't as comfortable as Gemma would have liked. She wasn't used to feeling self-conscious. And she really wasn't used to feeling aware like this around a guy.

She made herself stand still, her arms and hands relaxed at her side. She might have sent mental thanks to Seth for forcing her to perfect the skill in total self-defense. She'd sure learned to show no weakness or emotion around him.

It was as if little sparks were jumping from nerve ending to nerve ending. It didn't change anything, particularly knowing he and Ruth were obviously suspicious about something related to them, or peripherally because of Blaine.

Dan cleared his throat and Gemma gave it up as a bad job, trying to remember to call him agent.

"Would you like to sit?" she asked. She felt the need to sit and was relieved when he nodded. He waited for her to sit before he did, which was nice. Gallant even.

With conscious effort, she relaxed into the chair, not slumping but not bolt upright either. Her arms dangled from both rests, not a visible twitch in sight. She pretended it was Seth across from her. Well, she tried.

"You realize we had to do background checks on all of you," he said.

Oh dear. But she still didn't twitch or start. She settled for a thoughtful nod. "Of course."

"There's not a lot about you online."

She met his gaze, knowing exactly what he'd see. Some color might have crept into her cheeks. Hopefully, he didn't notice, with his attention on the notebook he'd extracted from his jacket pocket.

"No online presence on any of the social media sites?"

She gave a half shrug. "It's a privacy thing. And it cuts down on spam."

"True." He looked down again. "Smith & Jones. The firm focuses on efficiency?"

She nodded. Normally, this is where she'd add that she was just a secretary or sometimes she was a personal assistant, but she found she didn't want to lie to him. Things were going to get tricky if he really started digging.

Not because he'd find anything, but because he'd find very little.

His gaze returned to his notebook but before he could ask his next question, Ruth and Little Abner came up.

"I got a call from the local LEOs. We need to meet them."

Dan looked surprised, stowed his notebook and got up. "Thanks for your help," he said.

She was left staring at Little Abner.

"He left most of his stuff," he told her.

"So he did plan to come back." She had a bad feeling Blaine

wasn't coming back. She also had a feeling that Dan and Ruth would be back.

That she kind of hoped they would might be a problem.

* * *

The empty pirogue slowly emerged into view out of the deepening shadows. Prow up, it rested on a small island of semi-solid ground.

Dan and Ruth had switched to one of the sheriff's boats for the trip into the swamp. Then the small flotilla had made its way on a course that looked and felt random to Dan, but it had led them here, so maybe not that random.

The local guy who'd found the pirogue and reported it was in their boat.

The boat driver edged them closer to the pirogue, and Dan felt a chill run down his spine that was in direct odds with the intense humidity and heat.

"Told you it is Ledet's pirogue," their local said.

The various sheriff's deputies in the two boats exchanged unhappy looks.

The hull looked to be intact and there were no obvious signs of a problem. It just looked it had been pulled up and left. Except there was nowhere to go on foot from here, that Dan could see.

They drew in and one of the deputies got a hook on the pirogue and pulled it clear, so that it bumped gently against the side of their craft.

Now Dan could see the lone boot lying askew on the bottom. Insects buzzed around it and settled back as the movement eased off. What were they—his thoughts stopped at the sight of the brown splotches on the wood and on the boot.

"He'd never leave his boot behind," the local muttered.

"You're sure it's his boot?" The deputy sounded skeptical.

"He loved those boots. See those scrapes? Gator tried to bite him. That boot saved him."

Dan didn't look at Ruth, instead directing his attention to the surrounding area—at least what he could see in the rapidly lowering light. As a crime scene, this was less than ideal.

Green and slimy crap surrounded the pirogue and more was already trying to crawl up the sides and get inside. It wasn't a good idea to stop moving in this place. It liked to take back what it could and it didn't waste time doing it.

"We'll have to test for blood," the deputy said, rubbing sweat from his dripping brow.

It didn't help.

The only way to get rid of swamp sweat was to get out of the swamp into air conditioning and take a shower. Or two.

"I hate the swamp," Ruth muttered for his ears only.

Dan couldn't disagree. He hadn't joined the coast guard, or CGIS, to take swamp tours. But life was ironic like that.

Someone turned on the big lights and began moving the beams slowly across the boat and then the area around it.

Dan got out his phone and took pictures, both of the pirogue and the surrounding area. He wasn't sure who would ultimately have jurisdiction over this one, but he needed to assume it would be them for now.

Ledet was a local. Blaine wasn't. And the blood didn't mean either or both were dead. For right now, they'd be listed as missing.

"How far is this from Ledet's hunting camp?" Ruth asked.

The local peered around, like he didn't know this area like the back of his own hand, then gestured further up the swamp.

"Mebbe two mile."

Dan really wanted to let the locals take this one, but it was troubling that they weren't that far from where they'd found Perkins' body. He only knew this because of the GPS on his cellphone.

He wasn't sure where Ruth—or the powers-that-be on both sides—would come down on this one. And they'd all be involved in the search, he reminded himself. That was ironic, too.

It didn't surprise him when their boat turned in the direction of Ledet's camp. It was the next logical step.

One of the airboats in their group turned back, probably towing the pirogue to be processed.

Now they had to use their lights to navigate. The sky wasn't completely dark overhead, but the low hanging sun couldn't penetrate the dense growth.

It wasn't long before a dock loomed up out of the shadows. The camp was in a clearing so Dan could see the outlines of the cabin, touched with orange and gold from overhead light.

They tied up their boats, pulled out flashlights and went cautiously up the dock. It felt solid enough under foot, but Dan kept remembering the gap in the last one. He pulled up his GPS again and compared it to their current location.

They were uncomfortably close now, though dense swamp separated them, making "close" a concept more than a reality.

As they drew closer, Dan could see that the door hung crookedly open. Some glances were exchanged and then somehow Dan and Ruth were leading the way and the first to flash their lights inside.

It was a single room, so it didn't take long to realize there weren't bodies, but the room had been ransacked.

Ruth's light found a pool of darkening blood and then traced it to the door. They both stepped out and found it continued into the swamp for a few steps.

So someone had left alive but bleeding?

"The Rougarou," the local said, his voice hushed as he glanced fearfully around.

* * *

It was close on midnight when the other two airboats emerged from the dense dark of the swamp into the moonlight running along the surface of the lake.

The earlier boat had brought the pirogue back, but neither she nor Little Abner had been close enough to see more than an outline before it had vanished back into the dark. Gemma figured they were taking it to the sheriff's office for processing.

All three boats had been from the Terrebonne Sheriff's Office. But over their radio they'd heard the call going out for search and rescue help.

"Surely it's too dark," Gemma began then heard them say the search would start at dawn.

"You should get some sleep," Little Abner told her at one point. Instead she went and got them both food and water. She brought extra in case Ruth and Dan came back.

She didn't know why she was so certain they would.

The food was leftovers from the catering company that she'd split with Fred. Gemma ate it because it was good and because she needed to eat. She might regret it later. Her stomach was tightening from slowly increasing worry.

She wished she knew what to be worried about. She half turned to Little Abner to ask him if they should call someone. He would have an emergency contact number and there was Ashley—but she didn't because what did they have to tell anyone?

Blaine was overdue. The pirogue he'd been in had been found. That was all.

So she waited, they waited for further news.

"You should try to get some sleep," Little Abner said again. "Tomorrow will be a long day."

She almost asked him how he knew this, and almost told him she couldn't, but the sound of engines broke the silence.

"It might not be them," Gemma said, standing and going to the lake side with Little Abner.

First one airboat, then another, cruised into the moonlight. It looked like the same boats. She couldn't see the insignia in the dark.

One of them turned in the direction the earlier one had gone. The other nudged in next to the *Reel Escape*. Without a word, Little

Abner accepted the rope tossed their way and secured it. Gemma watched Dan and Ruth once again climb aboard.

The lighting was low, but it was clear that both Ruth and Dan were tired and hot.

She signaled for their driver to come, too and he did so eagerly. His uniform proclaimed him a deputy.

She led them first to the galley and got them cold water, then started handing them the rest of the catered food. They deserved better than cold cereal or a bologna and raisin bread sandwich.

She told herself to wait to ask questions, but then realized she didn't know what to ask anyway.

chapter five

Dan felt life returning to his body as he wolfed down the food and guzzled water until he almost drowned himself. They'd had water with them, of course, but it hadn't stayed cold.

This was icy and he almost moaned with relief.

Ruth ate more decorously, but she also made sure she got her share of the food.

The deputy wolfed his portion.

It had to be leftover from the catered lunch. He'd recognize Sarah's cooking anywhere.

He finally slowed, and then stopped, sitting back as tired replaced hunger and thirst.

He wanted to face plant somewhere. It didn't matter where. He wanted to get prone, stretch his legs, arms, and back. But he was also aware of Gemma and Little Abner, off to one side watching them in admirable silence.

He looked up, trying to think of something to say.

"We heard on the radio," Gemma said. "They're both missing."

He nodded.

"I need to head back to headquarters," the deputy said. It was clear he didn't know what to do with them.

"I didn't go into Blaine's room," she said, "but I did change the sheets in the room Ashley used. You can flip for the room or the couch. If you don't want to travel any further tonight?"

"That sounds great," Dan said and thanked the deputy, for doing his job, he vaguely guessed. He waited until the airboat had pulled away before speaking again.

"You take the bed," he told Ruth and almost felt his way to the couch, his eyelids were so heavy.

He was vaguely aware of the lights dimming, footsteps moving away.

He waited for darkness to close over his head and found he couldn't quite come all the way down.

He almost groaned. He and Ruth hadn't talked about what they learned from their team about Gemma or Little Abner. They hadn't been alone long enough at any point. He knew she'd found the information on Gemma as concerning as he did. He'd seen it in the way her brow creased as she read through the report.

His eyeballs felt like sandpaper, but he kept his lids firmly in place. He should be asleep. He would be asleep soon. Tomorrow would be time enough to try to figure out that puzzle of facts around Gemma that didn't fit what his eyes saw, what his instincts felt.

She hadn't finished college.

Smith & Jones claimed she was a secretary. A minor one at that.

But here she was on this Hatteras 54. Granted, she only owned half of it, but how did a minor secretary get several months off to cruise around the Gulf?

And then there was the fact that her clear-eyed and intelligent gaze didn't track with drop-out, secretary. He could see her starting there, but not staying there. He could see her as an efficiency expert. There was a calm competence about her that would be a bonus when telling people they needed to straighten up and fly right.

She could do it without them even knowing she'd done it, he thought with the tired remnants of a grin.

He rolled onto his back, covering his eyes with his arm.

But he could still see her watching him. He could still see her in his mind's eye.

Deep, way deep out of the past, he heard his stepmom's voice. "Go to sleep. Things will look better in the morning."

So he did. Though he wasn't sure anything would look better. Well, he was sure Gemma would look good.

***

Gemma woke to a not-unfamiliar tangle of images and thoughts.

It's not your job, she reminded herself. It was her problem, maybe, but not her job.

Dan and Ruth were both fully capable of sorting this mess out.

Seth wouldn't like that they'd checked on her. That popped to the front of her mind, but she didn't linger there. Seth didn't like much.

There were—and had been—definite signs that someone was trying to dig through the layers of the company, which might explain Seth's weird behavior, she supposed. She wished she believed herself.

Because the earlier digging couldn't have been Dan. So who had been digging into the company's secrets? Who else had been trying to find out more about her?

It wasn't unusual for hostiles to try to get at Enigma. Of course, the Coast Guard wasn't a hostile, but that's not how Seth would see it. But if he tried to recall her now, well, that would just raise more suspicions.

She pulled out her laptop and logged in and immediately a message popped from him.

Sit tight. We're working on back building your cover.

So he already knew she couldn't leave. He probably knew more than her. It was his superpower.

And she, he'd told her once, was his kryptonite.

She wasn't sure what that meant. She wasn't sure she ever would.

Seth *was* Enigma. And he was an enigma.

So she worked hard to make sure he only got to see her outside. What went on inside her head was her business not his.

An image of Dan popped into her head, but she stowed her laptop—and the image—away. She had no desire to probe her own mind right now either.

She found Ruth, Dan, and Little Abner, in the galley bravely eating the usual breakfast fare. She hid a smile at the sight of Ruth eating Froot Loops. The smell of coffee made her wrinkle her nose. She preferred to get her caffeine from a cold drink.

She popped the can's top and sat down in the only empty seat —next to Dan. She had no choice but to rub shoulders with him and kept her gaze directed down as she sipped.

Little Abner cleared his throat, and she gave him an inquiring look.

"They found Ledet not far from his hunting cabin," he told her. "Found him as soon as it got light enough to see."

"Blaine?"

He shook his head. "They are still looking."

"We need to search Blaine's room," Ruth said, her tone a mild contrast to the words.

Gemma supposed they'd only taken a cursory look last night. She had thought about searching it herself in the night, just to get ahead of anything that might compromise the *Reel Escape*. Only it didn't feel right. If Dan found out…

She squeezed off the thought. She probably had enough trouble with what they thought they knew about her.

They both rose and headed down. She might have followed them to the top of the shallow steps down, noting they were pulling on gloves. With an abrupt movement, she turned and went out onto the deck. From here she could see the search boats traversing the area around the bayou, while others—the smaller boats—headed back into the swamp.

Where was Blaine? She couldn't imagine him surviving in there all night but that presupposed he hadn't met someone. Ashley'd had plenty of time to arrange something. As had St. Cyr.

Gemma considered the mob guy. He didn't look or act like someone interested in investing in reality television. Was he hoping to launder money through the possible show? That seemed like a stretch. Blaine maybe had some footage and hope. That wasn't a show by any stretch yet.

But if there was something valuable out there? He'd probably want to be in on that. He might even be funding Blaine's "research."

Would Dan or Ruth find any of that so-called footage? Or had Ashley taken it with her? She claimed to be his film editor, so it was possible.

She propped her elbows on the railing and sighed. Had Blaine left anything of significance behind down there? Or was it all just for show?

At least she'd got this week's money upfront.

* * *

Blaine's stateroom was clearly the largest on the *Reel Escape*. The bed might have been a queen, Dan wasn't sure. The space had a cheerful look despite the spartan built-ins and air of stepping into the past.

Dan wasn't sure why, though it perhaps had to do with the age of the boat. Late eighties. The bedding and curtains had obviously been refreshed from the original. He gave a mental grimace, blaming the thought on his numerous sisters. You heard something long enough and pretty soon you were thinking it.

To clear his thoughts, he opened the door to the small head. A shaving kit sat on the edge of the sink and the seat was up. He unzipped the kit and did a quick rummage through the contents. It looked like everything a guy required was in there.

It didn't mean he'd planned to come back. Everything in there was also replaceable.

He turned back to the stateroom where Ruth was carefully going through the drawers. There wasn't much to see in them, or in the small closet. Again, just enough stuff to leave the impression he intended to return.

It wasn't a surprise his portable cameras weren't there. He'd have needed them for filming. But, if he had a laptop, it wasn't here. Not something you'd take into the swamp with you, he thought, though Blaine wasn't from the bayou. He made a mental note to ask if he'd had a laptop and if they'd seen him leaving with it, if he did.

Dan pushed back the clothes and found a suitcase tucked in the back. It wasn't exactly hiding. From what they'd said, Blaine had been aboard for at least three weeks. Made sense to unpack and then push the suitcase out of sight.

"No sign of any film," Ruth observed, straightening from checking out the lowest drawers. "Do they still use film?"

Dan shrugged. "I have no idea." If he'd been using a Go-Pro type device, then the film would probably be digital. "Miss Hammond may have taken it."

He checked the upper shelves, then lifted the suitcase out of the closet, noting the shift of something inside.

"There's something in here," he told Ruth.

While he worked the latches, Ruth turned to take a call.

"Right, thanks for the heads up," she said, turning back as he lifted the lid.

Inside was one of those portable file holders, with a band holding it closed. They both stared at it, Dan wondering if it was within their purview to look inside. Blaine was a lawyer. There might be confidential client documents inside.

"They found Blaine," Ruth said, her gaze lifting to meet his.

Dan didn't have to ask if he were alive. It was obvious he wasn't.

"He had the same kind of injuries as Perkins."

Dan sighed. That ought to ramp up the Rougarou rumors another notch. At this rate, the locals would be out with pitchforks and torches. Or the swamp equivalent of them.

"Did Ledet have similar injuries?" Dan asked.

"They said he did."

That was curious. Dan indicated the folder. "We gonna open it?"

"While I video record," Ruth said, holding up her cellphone.

"Go ahead." she said.

Dan slipped off the band holding it closed, careful not to block Ruth's view.

He opened the top, giving her a view of the tabs of several folders inside.

One looked like it might be a client folder, so he set that aside for now. He thumbed through the others, but none of them were labeled "St. Cyr."

There was one labeled "show." Inside he found notes for different episodes. He laid them out on the bed for Ruth to record.

"Maybe he was serious about the show," Dan muttered.

Ruth might have snorted, a female version of one anyway.

There were two more possible client folders. He set these with the other one and extracted the last folder.

"No label," he said. He exchanged another look with Ruth.

She hesitated, then nodded. "Let the record show that the folder lacked a clear identifying label. If the contents indicate privileged information, we will cease examining it."

He set it by itself on the end of the bed and opened it, so that it lay flat.

Ruth leaned in.

"That looks like a birth certificate," she said.

"Personal documents, maybe?" Dan mused, pulling the birth certificate clear of the other papers. He assumed it was Blaine's.

It wasn't.

It was Gemma Bailey's birth certificate.

* * *

If they were still searching, they were being very quiet. Not at all like TV and movie searches, though now that she thought about it, it was the way bad guys searched, by throwing things around.

It felt safer to mull this than worry about what they might find. If they found evidence of criminality, what then?

Little Abner came out onto the deck.

"Any news?" she asked.

"They found something, but then it went quiet," Little Abner said. "Could have been a false alarm."

Or they weren't ready to make it public. Gemma wasn't naive, even if Little Abner was clearly trying to protect her.

"Do you think he took off?" Had the presence of the two agents rattled him?

Little Abner shrugged. "Anything's possible. I'd be relieved if…"

She wasn't surprised he hadn't finished that sentence.

They sat quietly, but she heard only the occasional shuffle from below. She glanced at her phone. At least twenty minutes had passed. She hadn't noted the time right when they went down, but it seemed like a long time to search such a small stateroom.

She did a mental check list. Yeah, not much there.

A further five minutes passed before she heard the distinctive sound of the stateroom door opening and then closing.

There was a longer pause she couldn't figure out. She'd think they were standing there talking, but they'd have at least heard a murmur of that.

Finally, there was the sound of footsteps.

She knew exactly where they were and when they'd appear. She had grown up on this boat, after all.

When they came into view, Gemma felt a chill. It wasn't so much a change in expression but their body language. A new wariness and something more.

Ruth was a bit behind Dan, which felt weird. She'd had the impression Ruth was the team's leader. And he was a gentleman.

"Could we have a few words with you, Gemma?" Dan asked.

The careful tone increased her unease.

"Sure." Had they found out about Enigma somehow? No, that couldn't be it. They'd been searching Blaine's quarters, not hers.

But the hair on the back of her neck rose.

Little Abner followed them inside the small salon. She noted both of them hesitated, and then apparently decided not to object.

Ruth sat down at the small dining table, indicating Gemma should sit, too. That Dan didn't sit did not help. She'd liked his height until now, with him towering over her.

Not that Ruth's intent gaze wasn't unnerving enough for the moment. She sensed Little Abner hovering protectively behind her.

Ruth pushed a piece of paper across to her. A birth certificate.

Gemma picked it up and stared at it, but found it wasn't processing—at least, she could tell what it was, but not why she was being asked to look at it.

She lowered it, looked at Ruth, then at Dan, and then, with a shrug, set it down in front of her.

"It's my birth certificate," then added, "it's a copy." She gave a 'so what' shrug.

"It was in Blaine's papers," Dan said.

Gemma thought about this for a few seconds, hoping her brain would come online better.

"Well, that's creepy." She thought about it some more and decided that was all she had.

She sensed Little Abner shifting behind her.

"Look at it again, Gemma," Ruth said.

She frowned but picked it up and tried to look like she was looking again. She'd seen her birth certificate multiple times through the years.

She dropped it again. "What?"

Ruth's brow creased a little. "It says 'father unknown.' I thought Harry Bailey was your father?"

"In every way that matters, he was," Gemma said evenly. There were some holes in her past, even Enigma hadn't been able to fill—that she knew of, she amended. Seth didn't like holes, but he didn't share until it suited him.

The woman whose name was on that birth certificate was dead. She did know that.

Gemma had no memories of her mother. She'd been told she'd died. She hadn't challenged this, even though she was pretty sure it wasn't true. Even as a kid she'd been good at body language and tones in voices. There'd always been something in Fish's voice when he talked about her mother. She'd never been able to figure out why it made her uneasy.

It frustrated her, because that was kind of her superpower—following those niggles and gut nudges until knowledge unfolded before her.

She'd finally decided that maybe she didn't want to know. Denial wasn't her usual go-to place, but it was also true that Fish and Little Abner had been her only family. It would have been stupid to break what she had for a niggle or a nudge.

And now Fish was gone. If there had been a secret, he'd taken it with him to the grave.

She looked at the certificate again, though there was nothing new there. *Abigail Newton*.

The name brought no memories to mind and only a sun-blurred picture of a woman standing on the deck of a boat that Fish had given her—not the *Reel Escape*, though. The woman was shading her eyes with her hand, but one thing was certain, the hair blowing in the wind was blonde.

That didn't mean she wasn't Gemma's mom. The genetics of red hair were kind of complicated.

But she also knew she'd asked to see a picture and Fish produced a picture. It could have been anyone, though she'd taken it at face value at the time.

She'd been young.

Little Abner's hand came to rest on her shoulder.

"He loved you like his own."

She covered his hand with hers and gave it a squeeze. "I know."

That was actually the one certainty in her life. Fish had loved her. And that was probably the other reason she'd never rocked the boat.

Of course, there was that other thing, the also almost unacknowledged thing. She'd always felt like he'd had good reasons for what he never said.

She'd been through a lot of "I just want to know the truth" scenarios in her work and the "I just want to know" had turned to a pile of brown stuff and lots of regret when they found out the truth.

The truth could set one free if one really wanted the truth, not just to have their truth officially confirmed.

She fingered the edges of the birth certificate. It looked the same as the one in her personal files. So why did she feel like this one carried some of that brown stuff with it?

She gathered herself in and tapped the certificate with a finger tip. "I don't see why this matters." Matters to either of them was what she meant.

Ruth set a single page in front of her now. It looked like some kind of lab results.

She didn't pick it up.

She knew she had to.

She felt the fire under her toes, and her insides shifted into Shadow. She keep her gaze lowered because she didn't want Dan to see this side of her. She'd been told it was unsettling.

"It's the results of a DNA test," Ruth said, perhaps to fill the silence or to speed this along?

Maybe a bit of both.

She finally picked it up and read it in one swift glance. But she pretended it took her longer.

Even Shadow had trouble keeping her balance as it sunk in what this report claimed.

According to this, she shared DNA with Raymond Blaine, Sr. It also asserted that it was ninety-five percent likely he was her birth father.

How the freaking blazes had they got ahold of her DNA? If they had.

Shadow was skeptical. Gemma wanted to hyperventilate. Gemma was also outraged over the possible breach of her privacy.

She checked the date on the report and felt a sense of shock.

It had been done ten years ago.

Ten years? What had she been doing ten years ago? Even she couldn't remember right now.

And why had Blaine had it in *his* files?

Outrage surged again, but it faded quickly. What was the point? She already knew he wasn't a good guy.

And he was missing.

She glanced at Ruth through her lashes and felt certainty wash over her.

Blaine was dead.

Shadow kept Gemma steady as they both tried to figure out what it all meant.

She knew her face gave nothing away and they couldn't see her eyes. She wished she could see Dan. Or not. Maybe she didn't want to look into his eyes right now.

And…so what if Raymond Blaine's father was her sperm donor?

But it did cast a weird and possibly ugly light over him picking the *Reel Escape* for his trip.

She wanted to think about that, but the fire was still licking at her toes.

"What does it say?" Little Abner asked.

She handed him the sheet over her shoulder, still without letting Ruth see her eyes.

He read it and then said a few of the words she'd been thinking.

And there was that niggle. She twisted around, grateful for the respite from Ruth's gimlet gaze.

"Did you know?"

He avoided her gaze. "Not exactly. It was all so long ago…" His voice trailed off. "Fish was going to tell you himself."

Gemma knew her personal math. She was thirty-five for Pete's sake. And Fish hadn't found an opportunity to mention this in all that time? Anger, betrayal burned in her gut and she tamped them down. This was not the right time.

There might not be a right time. Fish was gone. This wasn't Little Abner's fault.

"He shouldn't have been able to find out," Little Abner muttered.

That made some questions try to bubble up. She pushed them back down, too. She took a slow breath, one designed not to show on the outside. And then she layered Gemma over the top of Shadow. Only then did she look at Ruth.

"I don't see how this is your business." Her voice came out with calm curiosity. If she'd had time and space, she'd have been pleased by that.

"If I'd known," Little Abner spluttered and then he touched her shoulder as if he expected her to shrug him off. She didn't and he squeezed, perhaps hoping it would provide comfort. Or support.

Holding Gemma's gaze, like a conjurer in a sideshow, Ruth produced more papers out of her hat—well possibly from her lap since she didn't have a hat.

There was just enough of the heading visible for her to see that it was a last will and testament.

What the heck?

Gemma had a bad feeling about this. So did Shadow.

Why had Blaine sought her out? Because he had to have chartered the *Reel Escape* because she was on it. What was his end game? He'd never asked her a single question about her past, her present, or even her future.

He hadn't even seemed to notice her particularly. Which was a bit peculiar now that she thought about it. Most of their charters spent a little time trying to find out if she was Little Abner's girl on the side.

To her it seemed so obvious, but she let them think what they wanted.

There was, however, no way around this. She'd have to go through it.

She picked the pages up as if they mattered not at all.

It was indeed a will. It took her a moment to realize it was Raymond Blaine's father's will. He could have given his son one name that was all his own, she thought with annoyed detachment.

This document took longer to go through.

She started through it, taking longer than she needed to buy some time.

It was an interesting, if disturbing read.

If she died in suspicious circumstances, Raymond Blaine Junior, would be disinherited. If she died in any circumstances, his inheritance would be severely reduced.

So the old man outed her, but was afraid his son would have her killed? He could have kept his big mouth shut and saved them all a lot of trouble. So why hadn't he?

She reached that part and managed to not suck in a breath thanks to Shadow. Gemma wanted to blink like an owl.

If Blaine Junior died under any circumstances, she inherited everything.

She half frowned because that wasn't a giveaway. Her credit check of Blaine Junior's finances made her wonder if there was anything for her to inherit if he did die.

See, she should always do the deep background check. It wouldn't have helped her with the DNA thing, but she'd have had a better idea of the scum at the bottom of Blaine Junior's soul.

And she wouldn't have been so flat-footed right now about who and what Blaine Senior was.

She lifted her gaze to meet Ruth's once more—it was time and she felt again that deep certainty that Blaine Jr. was dead.

And that she had a very good motive for his murder.

chapter six

Dan felt the difference in Gemma without being able to figure out why. Her face hadn't changed. She'd weathered the various shocks rather well, he'd noted.

She'd kept her expression locked down, but no one could control the paling or flushing of their skin. She'd definitely lost color more than once.

He didn't like that this gave him hope.

He didn't like this, any of it, at all. Like the swamp so close by, there was a murk and mire beneath what should, and kind of was, a placid surface. He didn't think the murk came from her.

She'd gone quiet, as if she'd realized she could be a suspect. *Was a suspect*, he told himself. She had to be, though when he drilled down, it all became more amorphous.

They had *a* will, but they didn't know if it was a legal will or even the last will. They didn't know that Blaine Sr. had anything to leave to anyone.

Money on paper could evaporate like mist.

His thoughts jolted to a stop.

They didn't know if Blaine Sr. was dead.

Ruth looked at him, as if the same thought, or one close to it, had occurred to her.

"I'm going to call the team and find out some things," she said.

Gemma didn't move, but her gaze did a quick shift between them before returning to the will sitting in front of her.

Her hands rested on the table on either side of the papers, neither twitching nor unnaturally still.

Ruth left, and after a hesitation, Dan sat down in her seat.

Why had Abner Abbot said that? That question felt like mud bubbling up from a deep depth. Why had they tried to hide who Gemma was? Just how had they accomplished it—if they had? The DNA test was ten years old.

Did Gemma really not know? If she had, it put a bad light on them taking the charter.

But it didn't look like she knew. Or she was a world class actress who could change color at will.

On paper she was a college drop-out and a minor secretary. But looking at her right now? He knew in his gut there was more to her story than that.

One sentence came back to him.

They weren't supposed to be able to find out.

What had Abbot meant by that?

"Have a seat," he told Abbot.

He wasn't as good as Gemma at hiding his feelings. He looked troubled, his eyes sick with worry.

"She didn't know," he said.

Dan glanced at Gemma and had to agree, but their belief wasn't going to help clear her just yet.

Blaine's time of death might help. He and Ruth had been aboard with them since early evening yesterday.

But they only had Gemma and Abbot's word that Blaine had actually left, since Ledet was dead, too.

Ledet. Somehow thinking his name eased a tightness he'd hadn't been aware was there.

It was a bit of a stretch to think these two could overpower

Pirogue Wipeout

both men. Unless Ledet's task was to get rid of Blaine? Or they'd overpowered them one at a time?

That felt like a stretch. Abbot was a sturdy old man, but he was still an old man. In his seventies, if he recalled correctly what they'd learned about him.

He glanced around. This was a yacht but not a luxury one. It had been well-kept but nothing fancy had been added to it, at least nothing that he'd noticed when they'd boarded the first time.

It was what it had been: a mid-range sailing vessel for lower end charters.

Blaine Junior had been a lawyer, but that didn't mean he had a lot of money. Making it wasn't always the hard part. Keeping it? That was a challenge for a lot of people.

Money.

When their dead Coastie had gone missing had there been something more than that mysterious passenger on board? Were the quiet rumors true? But why wait so long, if that's what Perkins had been doing here?

From the file compiled at the time, with the relevant data forwarded to his phone, they knew the woman seen entering the small plane had her hair covered and could have been in her mid-thirties.

That wasn't much to go on, it had been so little in fact that she'd never been identified. It was curious no family had come forward, and none of the missing persons reports at the time had produced a credible lead to her identity.

If there had been something, something valuable or just old and dangerous information, St. Cyr was a much more likely co-conspirator than Gemma or Abbot.

They needed to find out where he'd been since he drove away —though he wouldn't have done it himself. Wise guys had people who killed for them.

His thoughts circled back to Gemma, and he realized she was studying him with a profoundly enigmatic expression.

He gave himself an inner shake. He needed to act like an

investigator not—well, he wasn't sure how he was acting. He looked at his notes and grabbed a question from them.

"Did Blaine have a laptop when he came on board?"

Even Gemma blinked at this apparent change in subject.

She frowned. "Ashley mentioned needing to do some edits on their film. Maybe she took it." Gemma added, "You know I don't think I ever saw him working on a laptop, just using his phone."

They had people looking for Ashley Hammond. And as far as he knew, Blaine's cellphone hadn't been recovered yet.

"Did she say why she was leaving?"

Gemma half shrugged. "I think she was tired of sitting around waiting for him to get his footage. We don't exactly have luxury accommodations or provisions."

He arched a brow at this.

"I'm not much of a galley cook," she explained. "We do make that clear before anyone signs anything."

"That's right," he said, "you're a…secretary?"

She nodded.

That didn't preclude the ability to cook, but he knew from his sisters—and his brothers—the ability to turn provisions palatable was a random skill set.

"That's why he had his meal with St. Cyr catered." It made a bit more sense now. It must have cost Blaine something to have the meal brought down here. If he had? "Did Blaine pay for the catering service?"

"We sure wouldn't," Abbot said, with a huff. "Our contract was week-to-week, cash up front."

Dan glanced at Gemma. That didn't seem quite standard.

"His credit check was a little suspicious," she said.

"I tried to wave him off," Abbot said. "Probably the most unfriendly contract we've ever put together. I didn't like the cut of his jib," he added, as if Dan had asked. "I didn't know…the other."

"What did you know?" Dan posed the question casually, but his gaze homed in on the old man.

"About Fish?"

Dan nodded.

"We'd been friends since school. He showed up one day with this idea to buy a boat and do charters."

"How did you arrange the financing?"

Abbot's fingers tapped the top of the table for a few seconds. "He had his half. I financed my half."

"And the four of you lived on here?" Maybe they hadn't taken overnight charters?

"It was just me and Fish for a few months."

He glanced at Gemma, but as far as Dan could tell he got no help from her.

"One day he told me he had to leave for a couple of days. When he came back, he had Gemma with him."

Gemma gave no sign this might be news to her, but Dan still had the impression it was, perhaps because of the way Abbot kept looking at her.

She didn't look at him, just sat there with her lashes hiding her gaze. Her body language showed no sign of tension, not even a finger twitch.

"He didn't tell you what happened to Gemma's mother?"

"He said she'd died or was dying, I don't rightly recall now. It just was."

"You never tried to find out anything more?"

"If Fish had wanted me to know, he would have told me."

That was a lot of trust. Did he believe him? Dan wasn't sure. He glanced at his notes again and tried to think how to ask the next question. He quickly realized there wasn't a good way to ask it.

"You said Miss Hammond had her own stateroom." He knew this type of boat only had three, and for the first time he wondered where she and Abbot had been bunking.

"As far as I know," Gemma said, with a flicker of a smile, "she used it. We were just glad she left so we didn't have to keep bunking together."

Her quick grin at Abbot seemed to relax him. And it seemed to indicate that what she'd heard hadn't been news to her.

"Little Abner snores," she added.

"I do not," Abbot retorted. "You're hearing yourself rattling the rafters."

"I have a very genteel snore. A girl snore."

This had the feel of an old "argument," the kind family had. They'd learned to cope when the charters pushed them into the crew spaces, which also felt of family. And they'd given up the stateroom for Ruth.

He looked down to hide a frown.

It didn't seem like two people trying to hide something. Or was it two people keeping them close, so they'd know what was going on?

Could Gemma have really recovered this quickly from what she'd learned about Blaine? Her color had mostly returned, though he thought he saw signs of strain around her eyes. He could be seeing them because he wanted to.

For a minute his breath froze at how much he didn't want her to be guilty of anything.

"Blaine is dead, isn't he?" she said.

He couldn't lie about it, so he nodded.

She didn't ask for details he couldn't give her.

"Both dead." Abbot said this as if talking to himself. He glanced up. "Thought if anyone could bring Blaine back alive it was Ledet."

A born and raised here Cajun wouldn't have lost his boot and his boat. Dan had known Ledet was dead before they found the pirogue.

"I trusted him, too," she agreed.

Trusted him? He must have given some sign of his surprise.

"To bring our charter safely back," she said. "It doesn't look good, even if it happens somewhere else. And the whole Rougarou thing?"

She rolled her eyes.

"Don't do that where people can see you," he cautioned, with a grin that might have surprised both of them. "Down here? We believe."

Her lips twitched. "Good to know."

* * *

When Ruth had returned, she'd politely requested that they cruise to Dulac, to the Coast Guard station there. They needed to understand, she'd said, that since Blaine's death was not a natural one, the *Reel* would need to be searched.

They'd been given time to grab their go-bags, but Ruth hadn't thought they'd need them.

Gemma knew they wouldn't find blood splatter and her worries about Blaine hiding something illegal had subsided some after they searched his stateroom.

Ruth had made sure that Gemma's laptop was indeed hers before allowing her to pack it in her bag.

Dan stayed on the flybridge with Little Abner while he figured out their course through the lake's channels. Little Abner didn't hurry.

He might have been hoping to annoy them.

He didn't like his feet being held to the fire anymore than she did.

She itched to get on her laptop and find out more about the man who seemed to think he was her biological father.

Would she contact Seth? She kept changing her mind. She didn't want him involved in this.

She liked to keep her private life—particularly this private life—separate from her job.

What she wanted was information without Seth's involvement. She needed access to the company's resources again.

Did she believe the DNA test results?

She wasn't sure.

DNA tests could be faked. She just couldn't see the why behind this one.

So many questions jostled her brain, so it was a good thing she wasn't at the helm.

Who? What? Why? Where? How?

And if Blaine Senior was her father, who was her mother? Did she even want to know?

And how the heck had Blaine Senior found out something she'd never found out about herself?

She had better resources. Well, Seth had better resources.

Of course, she hadn't really wanted to know. So there was that.

Little Abner's account of her arrival differed some from what Fish had told her. She'd always assumed that Little Abner had met her mother. Had they wanted her to have that impression?

All the certainties in her life suddenly seemed like a hall of mirrors and shadows and shifting realities.

The name on her birth certificate felt even more fake than usual. But it still stretched credibility to believe that, out of the blue, Blaine Senior had located her. The trail would have been long cold.

She knew, better than most, how cold trails could be.

If he had money—an unknown at the moment—he could have warmed up the trail, but why wait until now to contact her?

Okay, so Fish died last year.

But it wasn't like he was hiding all those years. She'd have blamed his obituary, but the test was ten years old. She stiffened. His picture. On the *Reel Escape's* charter website. That's what had happened about ten years ago. Both men had resisted a website for too long, counting on word-of-mouth to bring them charter clients.

That had to be it.

Facial recognition software had improved by more than leaps and bounds in the last thirty-five years. She should know. It was one of the tools in her arsenal at work. If it had been that, she couldn't overlook the irony.

Or it had been a weird coincidence. Those happened, too.

She went to the flybridge, either to escape her thoughts or to see Dan. She wasn't sure which drove her. He glanced at her when she came in, a flicker of a smile lighting his face before he looked away. She felt a little better as she settled on the small couch behind the helm.

The engines blurred the sounds of movement, but Gemma had good instincts and sensed when Ruth joined them on the flybridge.

She sat down next to Gemma.

"Are you all right?" Ruth asked, needing to raise her voice a little.

Gemma saw Little Abner's shoulders twitch, but he didn't turn around.

"It's a lot to process," she said. She didn't like admitting anything, but she also didn't want to get charged with murder. Shadow hovered watchfully just below the surface, but this was outside her experience, too.

She kept her gaze ahead, because it felt right, but the urge to look at Ruth to gauge her reaction was strong.

She was used to reading body language and adjusting, but she didn't dare to do that in front of someone who was probably as good at it as Gemma was.

"You really didn't know?" The question wasn't accusatory. It reminded Gemma of them chatting at lunch a million years—and two days ago.

Only two days. Oh my.

Gemma did some calculations, figured she could handle it, and drew a leg up, shifting so that one leg was tucked under and she half faced the agent.

She stepped one mental foot carefully on the wire.

"I always sensed there was something odd about my mother," she admitted. Because she was being honest, she was able to sound honest. It was always the better path.

"But you never tried to find out?"

Gemma let herself think about this. This was a natural thing to do, and it gave her time to frame her response.

"I thought about it." She leaned back and ran a hand over her face, pushing back some escaped strands of hair. Her face felt damp and was probably shiny.

"But you never did anything?"

"Once," she said, this time without hesitating. She was following her gut now about how to play this. *Play.* She almost snorted. Playing the truth. "I started to and I realized something."

She was back in the moment, looking at her father's face. As young as she'd been, she'd sensed or seen the red signal lights flashing all around him. *Do not enter.* Or—*enter at your own risk.*

She'd never know which now.

"It wasn't just a secret he was keeping." She sighed and looked directly at Ruth. "He was standing on a landmine. I felt it, even as a selfish and self-centered teen. And I just backed off."

It was the truth, an instinctive act of self preservation that she'd tried not to think of again. Because if she'd dwelt on it, it would have changed things between them. So she'd jumped over it. But now she remembered the relief in Fish's face.

She'd buried that, too.

There was a short silence, then Gemma spoke again. "This—Blaine and his father—doesn't feel big enough for what I remember." This instinct was stronger, fueled by the training she'd received for her job. She'd had the right gut reactions, but Seth's people had helped her hone them.

"You still believe something is going to blow up?" Ruth's tone was careful.

She probably didn't want to stop the flow. The trickle, Gemma amended the thought.

"Even more than I did back then."

* * *

Pirogue Wipeout

Dan watched as Gemma and Abbot docked the *Reel Escape*. It was clear they'd worked together for a long time.

Once the boat was secure, he and Ruth climbed onto the dock and turned to watch Gemma and Abbot—both carrying small go-bags—came ashore, too.

A young Ensign standing nearby, came forward at his signal.

"I'll take those," he said. "And we have a place for you to wait."

"Can we go find food?" Abbot asked. "I've been eating her grub for too long."

"Secure their gear for them, Ensign," Dan said. He looked at Abbot. "Let's go find you some food."

Now that he thought about it, he was hungry, too. He glanced at Ruth to see if she wanted to join them, but she gave a slight shake of the head.

He managed to borrow a Jeep and drove the three of them into Dulac.

Dan had been here before, so he knew where to go and soon they were seated at a wobbly table, covered by a plastic tablecloth. It smelled as good as he remembered, though.

Neither Abbot nor Gemma questioned the rustic surroundings. They focused on the menu and were ready when a waiter came for their orders.

Dan's phone trilled. He glanced at the screen and grimaced. "I'll have to take this."

He answered as he walked away. It was Ruth.

"Ledet has the same injuries as Blaine. The body was wearing the other boot."

Dan had been expecting this. A Cajun didn't give up their pirogue without a fight. Or their boots, for that matter.

"Foul play?"

"Probably. He's been in the water."

Dan didn't have to guess what that meant. He was glad he got to eat before he saw it, and didn't mind admitting to himself he'd rather pass seeing the corpse.

"Do you think they're involved?" Dan asked the question, knowing she'd know who he meant. He didn't think they were, but he wasn't sure he could trust his gut this time.

There was a long silence. "I don't," she said finally, "but there are secrets swirling around that girl."

Dan couldn't argue with that. He cut off the call and went back to the table.

Gemma watched him sit, then said, "Did they find something?"

Her tension wasn't surprising. Their boat could be impounded if it was proved they'd known about any illegal conduct.

He shook his head. "They aren't done yet. That was about something else."

She looked like she wanted to ask, but her lips compressed over the question.

He was grateful. He had the odd sense that he couldn't lie to her, that he needed to not lie to her.

Abbot took a drink of the soda that had arrived while Dan was taking his call.

Gemma's hand circled hers, but she didn't lift it up, just watched him across the table.

"Are we, am I, in trouble?"

"Not if you haven't done anything wrong." He forced himself to look into her eyes. Why did he feel guilty? He sure as heck hadn't done anything wrong. So why did he feel like he had?

"And you never get it wrong?"

"We're not perfect."

Her lips curved up on the edges. "No one is. It shouldn't be a crime."

Ignorance of the law was no excuse, but he was pretty sure that wasn't what she was talking about. Ruth's words came back to him.

"There are secrets swirling around that girl."

It almost seemed like he could see them, trailing wisps that danced and curled around her, hiding and then revealing her serious gray gaze.

And then the moment broke apart as their waiter arrived with the food.

Dan didn't remember what he ate, or what they ate. It wasn't fair to good food and when he was less—he groped for a word but the one that came made him blink because it was one his new stepmother used—discombobulated.

Discombobulated.

It fit, though if he had to spell it...When he was less that, he'd enjoy his food again.

This time his phone pinged with a text. Again, from Ruth.

Done. Boat clear. Ask them to remain in the area, though.

"You're cleared to go back to your boat," he told them, his gaze watchful, despite the guilt. "We'd like you to remain in the area to assist with our inquiries," he added.

Neither looked relieved or surprised. They nodded.

Abbot took their ticket from the server, giving Dan an ironic look. "Will it look like bribery if I pay this?"

"No, but..."

"It's easier than doing the math," Abbot said, handing over some cash.

So he didn't intend to let Dan pay for their food. Tough old coot, but Dan liked him. He kind of reminded Dan of a sea-going version of his dad. It was a relief they'd cleared one suspicion hurdle. He wished he knew how many were left.

"Sorry about all this," Dan said as they headed back to the Jeep.

"Life is unpredictable on the water," Gemma said.

He could only agree with her, but this wasn't the kind of situation anyone could prepare for ahead of time.

There wasn't a door to open, but he came around to help her into the back, leaving the front seat for Abbot. That his hands wanted to keep holding onto hers was a worry.

He met her gaze and noted a tiny flicker of something in there and his heart gave an odd jerk. But the wisps of secrets were there, too, swirling around her like swamp fog trying to hide her from his view.

Her lashes dropped over her eyes and when they lifted, she was back in neutral. He couldn't even call it wary. She'd just withdrawn. And the fact that he knew it? It kind of freaked him out.

He walked around and climbed behind the wheel with something that was all his crap surrounding him now. It felt and smelled like regret with a pervasive sense of missed opportunity.

Or he needed a shower.

It was probably that.

chapter seven

They found a berth at the marina for the *Reel Escape* in Dulac, though the fees made Gemma wince now that their cash flow had died.

It was a cold thought, and she sighed a bit at herself, but it was also their reality. They needed to pay for fuel, supplies, and fees to get back home. Where there would be fees and supplies.

"We should get a shorter boat," she'd said to Little Abner, who'd given her an affronted look.

At least she didn't have to cook.

Little Abner had managed to run into an old friend who he hoped would help him to scare up a fishing charter or two to help with the bills. Was it a loose interpretation of "don't leave town?" Possibly, but they needed the work.

She could have helped their cash flow, but Little Abner wouldn't let her put any of her own money into the boat.

It had taken her three times of pacing around the deck before she could sit down and contact Seth.

Because she couldn't see him, she couldn't get a sense of how much he knew. The upside was, he couldn't see her either.

This meant they danced around what had happened here. She kept it shy of facts, but in sight of the truth.

They'd had a problem with their charter and would be in Dulac for a few days.

It was nothing she couldn't handle.

It was nothing he needed to worry about.

Unless she was arrested for murder.

She didn't say that, of course. It was weird enough to think it.

She knew she hadn't killed anyone or done anything wrong.

She knew Little Abner hadn't killed anyone. She wasn't quite sure about the "anything wrong."

Her view of him had shifted since learning the secrets he'd kept.

She really hated it when the people in her life tried to "protect" her. It was such crap.

"Here's a thought," she muttered. "Just tell me and let me decide how I feel about it."

It was hard not to feel like Seth had known at least some of the secrets of her past. Knowledge was his favorite currency. If he'd known any of it...

The idea pissed her off so much, her hands clenched into fists.

Could he have forgotten she had red hair and all that came with it?

She might need to make sure he found out it wasn't just for show.

With that deck cleared as much as was possible, she switched to the research she'd been itching to do.

Raymond Blaine, Sr.

And she was totally using work resources for this.

* * *

Dan was aware of Ruth using the desk—and computer—next to his. He'd have preferred to be moving, either walking out the stitch in his back from the night on the couch, or on his Triumph with moving air on his face and an open road.

A hot shower had only gotten him halfway over it.

It hadn't helped at all with the stitch in his brain.

Who was Gemma Bailey?

Their best people had been digging in all the usual places. She'd appeared now and again on other people's social media, and one of the techs had found her in a picture from WHART, Wildlife-Human Attack Response Training.

It was, according to his source, a five-day course—part lecture and part field training—taught by the British Columbia Conservation Officer Service.

What the heck was a secretary doing taking a course like that?

The tech was trying to get him a list of attendees, but the group image was five years ago. It was going to take time.

Ruth's chair creaked as she leaned back and rubbed her face.

"So the emergency contact information that Abbot gave us was for Blaine's secretary, but here's the interesting part. His father is still alive."

Dan swiveled to look at her. "He is?"

"He's in his eighties, retired from a construction business. Was married. Wife is deceased. One son."

A now deceased son.

Dan resisted the urge to get up and look for himself.

"His reputation is better than his son's." She frowned and leaned closer to the borrowed computer screen. "And better than his wife's." She looked him. "She's a second cousin or something of St. Cyr."

This time he had to get up and look. He leaned over her shoulder. Whoever had assembled the data had done a good job. They'd kept digging until they found what looked like the bottom.

"So he's an upstanding citizen. She ran an import business." Dan frowned, looking at the date of the wife's death. It wasn't suspiciously close to Perkins and the others' disappearance. "She declared bankruptcy in 1988. Shut the business down and for all outward appearances, became a society wife."

"Was known for her philanthropic works," Ruth said, skeptically. "We need to talk to Blaine Senior."

"Does he even know about his son's death?" Dan wondered.

"That's a good question. We need to get some people over there." Ruth reached for her cellphone and Dan went back to his borrowed desk where the image from the WHART course was still pulled up.

Gemma had been in the front row, or he doubted the facial recognition software would have found her. The two back rows were much less distinct.

She looked serious and sober, wearing her WHART tee shirt and cap.

He tried zooming in on her, but the image quickly blurred. The quality wasn't good for much.

He leaned back, remembering her talking about them bringing someone in who'd been injured. Could it be some kind of weird hobby?

Ruth lowered her cellphone. "The local LEOs are going to send someone over to talk to him. It doesn't look like its hit the news there yet. From their attitude, he's respected, the son isn't."

They might make a good study for nature versus nurture.

The whole setup reminded Dan of the tree roots in New Orleans. The roots ran along the top of the ground because the water table was so high, but they intertwined with each other for support. That was how oak trees survived for hundreds of years.

The trees did it for strength in the storms. This didn't remind him of that.

It was more like hiding. The roots twisted and turned, sometimes hiding one beneath it, then emerging briefly to the surface.

They had three bodies, but he had the sense that they were only seeing a shallow surface. That so much more was going on just out of sight.

The wise guy, the boat captain, and the enigma. Which of them knew what? And how did it all connect?

There was no indication of a daughter going missing, so it seemed unlikely that Gemma was part St. Cyr.

He pulled up an image of Gemma's birth certificate with Abbot's words echoing in his head.

They weren't supposed to be able to find her.

Their tech had compiled enough data on the woman listed on the certificate for him to know two things.

That woman was dead.

That woman probably wasn't Gemma's mother's real name.

He let what they knew drift idly in the front of his mind, pulling up random facts here and there and seeing if they fit somewhere.

Inside his head, he could play "what if" and no one had to know. So…

What if the unknown woman on the plane with Perkins was Gemma's mother?

The timing fit, even he literally had nothing to go on but the fact it was a woman.

Bankruptcy.

The wife of Gemma's father is bankrupt less than a year later. The bankruptcy documents blamed a warehouse fire the year before.

Dan started sketching a timeline on a piece of paper.

The warehouse fire was close to the same time the plane went missing.

He made a note to see if they could get their hands on a list of what was destroyed in the fire.

And then he wrote a last question:

Who else on that missing plane was still alive?

* * *

Gemma hadn't expected to find out Raymond Blaine Senior was alive.

He even had a Wikipedia page.

It didn't take her long to learn he was considered an upstanding citizen, a pillar of his community.

That felt weird. She could admit to herself she'd been judging her bio-dad in the same frame as his legit son.

So what happened to Junior?

She needed to look at his wife's details, but she didn't want to. It made no sense. The woman was dead and couldn't be hurt by Gemma's existence.

It still felt wrong, as if Gemma were part of that old betrayal.

Was this some—or all—of the landmine Fish hadn't wanted her to find? It still didn't feel big enough for his level of unease.

She stared at her winking cursor, waiting for her to type in the next search, but instead of Mrs. Blaine's name, she typed in:

Harry Bailey, also known as Fish Bailey.

She wasn't sure why she'd never tried to find out anything about him, or his family. Had she taken him at his word that there was no one else? Or had she wrapped it all in the package she'd mentally labeled 'time bomb' and moved on?

She hesitated, then tapped return and closed her eyes. She counted to ten and opened them.

She had her first shock. And how did she know it was only the first?

He was born in Montana? He'd grown up land-locked, too? Had he and Little Abner known each other back then?

Parents, deceased.

She knew that. It was nice to know something was true.

Sister.

Wait, what? He'd had a sister?

None of them were public figures, so the search was harder, but this was Gemma's jam, it's what she did.

It felt harder even than expected this time, but she didn't know if the data was hiding, or her spirit was unwilling.

But in the end, she got it.

A picture of Fish's sister. It wasn't a great picture, but it was enough.

Fish wasn't her father. He was her uncle.

She stared at the pale image of herself for a long time.

She knew the next step. Facial recognition software.

It was the only way. The name on Gemma's birth certificate was a fake—or a new identity for Mary Bailey. And if she was still alive, she wouldn't be calling herself Mary or Bailey.

She wasn't sure why she closed her laptop without starting the process.

* * *

They'd stopped for lunch, just some sandwiches from the PX, when it hit Dan they'd missed a key area of research.

He yanked out his cellphone and sent the text to the tech.

Ruth looked up. "What?"

"Fish Bailey, her dad," he said.

She frowned, then her expression cleared. "You're right. We need to know more about him, too."

Ruth's cellphone trilled and she answered it. "Okay, thank you for your help." She lowered the phone. "Raymond Blaine, Senior is incoming."

"So he knows."

"He knows."

Dan took a couple of bites while he reflected—again—on the tangle that was this case.

They had three bodies, all of them officially identified—and one they still hadn't been able to trace back to the name he'd been using for the last thirty-six years.

And one body that was connected to Gemma. He didn't like that data point.

Ledet was probably a peripheral casualty, but they didn't know that for sure.

And now they had one definite connection between Blaine and St. Cyr.

It would be nice to know how it all fit together.

"This case is as messy as the swamp," Ruth said.

She didn't sound gloomy. That wasn't her style, but Dan thought he detected a hint of frustration in there.

Ruth was a bulldog, but there were too many trails to sniff out. Stinky trails, some of them.

She glanced at him. "There's a definite swirl of something around Gemma Bailey."

He couldn't argue with it, though he wanted to.

"Do you think she's in danger?" he asked. He still found it hard to believe she was some kind of ruthless killer.

"If one of our players thought she knew something?" Ruth pursed her lips, then finished, "She might be."

"Do you think she knows something?" Dan wasn't sure why he was pushing. Maybe it had to do with ripping band aids off quickly.

"I think she knows a lot of things," Ruth said.

Dan felt his gut twist.

"Do I think she knows anything that will actually help? I'm not sure. It may be that she doesn't know she knows."

So Ruth was fighting the same thing he was. It was kind of a relief to know she found Gemma puzzling—but not evil.

Now it was Dan's turn for his cellphone to ping an interruption. It was a text from the tech. He read it and looked up.

"Fish Bailey had a sister," he said. And he showed her the photograph that had arrived with the text.

Ruth's brows arched. "Well, well."

chapter eight

Gemma tried to stop pacing. It just made her hotter and sweatier. Finally she leaned against the canal side rail and stared down at the water.

Why didn't she want to know more about her mother?

It was the right question.

If she drilled down to what she did for Seth, it was simple. She found things out.

Why hadn't she ever tried to find out more about her mother?

It messed with who she thought she was and who she thought she wasn't—one of those river denial people.

What she felt right now? It felt a lot like denial.

"But I don't know anything," she muttered, "I don't even know enough to be afraid of what I'll find out."

She didn't mind finding out Fish was her uncle. There was an actual family tie there. And it made a lot of sense looking at back at how they'd interacted with each other. She'd never called him dad, only Fish.

So the door she didn't want to open only dealt with her mother.

Mary Bailey. She felt no more connection than what she'd had with the name on her birth certificate, no *aha* of discovery.

Maybe she was some kind of unnatural person, not quite a

vampire, but someone who should have been on Blaine's reality show.

The air was thick and hard to draw into her lungs. She looked up and saw storm clouds gathering off to the south.

She retreated to the salon and watched it sweep through, the drops of water hitting the deck with enough force to cause them to rebound an inch or so.

She leaned against the glass, watching until the clouds moved on. Already the water was beginning to steam off the deck.

The humidity would be worse, but she slid open the door, letting the damp wave wash over her as she stepped out into the open.

Her feet wanted to pace—

"Miss Bailey?"

The voice was not one she recognized. She crossed over to the dock side and looked down.

She immediately wished she hadn't.

Flanked by his two bodyguards, St. Cyr and Ashley stood on the dock, looking up at her.

She couldn't see the limo, but she wouldn't. The parking wasn't as close to the dock as their last encounter.

Funny to feel a sudden chill that should have been a welcome relief against the heat. It wasn't.

Ashley looked surprisingly expressionless. This break in her protocol upped the chill factor.

St. Cyr looked the same. Thin, gray and pale. His suit looked even more ludicrous here than it had before.

How could he stand wearing it in this heat?

"Can we come aboard?"

Gemma realized it was one of the bodyguards who asked the question. Apparently, St. Cyr had people to talk for him, too.

"I'll come down," she said, and turned away before anyone could protest.

She didn't want any of them onboard when she was alone or

Pirogue Wipeout

ever again. She hadn't removed her hat, but she did don her sunglasses before she reached the lower deck.

All four of them were waiting, not unlike statues. She felt the hint of humor ease the tension in her gut.

Having her eyes hidden helped with the creep factor and the hat helped with the heat—a little.

She jumped ashore and glanced around. There was a weather-beaten bench next to a piling.

"We can go over there and sit." She pointed.

St. Cyr blinked, then lifted a limp wrist to point at her boat.

She didn't speak, just waited for him to figure it out.

The arm lowered back to St. Cyr's side and he turned, walking to the bench. He looked down at it as if it might bite him.

It was not beyond the realm of possibility. It was in bad need of a sanding.

He pulled a handkerchief out of his breast pocket and handed it to one of the bodyguards.

The man bent and spread it over a spot at one end. Only then did St. Cyr sit down.

Gemma didn't look at Ashley, reminding herself one shouldn't expect good manners from a crime boss. And possibly he only had one handkerchief.

Before she could warn Ashley about the possible splinters, she took over the end furthest from St. Cyr.

Gemma decided that standing was better than occupying the illusionary middle ground between the two.

There was no middle ground here.

Gemma planted her feet and would have arched her brows, but her glasses were too big for them to see it. It was too hot for wasted effort.

She crossed her arms and let her chin angle into a hint of pugnacious.

St. Cyr looked past her to the *Reel Escape*.

"I was hoping to see Raymond."

Gemma blinked. Why hadn't he just said do? Seriously, dude?

Did he really not know? Did Ashley not know or wasn't she talking?

Ashely pulled sunglasses out of her handbag and put them on. As a distancing tactic, it was a bit effective,

St. Cyr's pale, gaunt face gave nothing away. It was as if it had given up trying to have expression.

She really didn't want to say it. She knew what could happen to messengers. This could also be a ploy to telegraph innocence.

She pursed her lips.

"He's surely back by now," Ashley said.

"He's back," Gemma said. "But he had an accident."

"Well, there's a shock," Ashley said, with a very ungenteel snort.

Was she really trying to cushion the news for the mob guy and the—she wasn't sure what Ashley was, now that she thought about it.

"Accident." The word came out slowly with no question to it. Maybe his voice had forgotten how to do inflection, too?

It had to be done, so she said it. "He's dead."

St. Cyr's face didn't change, though he did blink once. But that could have been the sun. He was almost looking into it because she could feel it beating down on her back.

Or was the blink a sign of extreme emotion?

"Dead." He didn't move, or signal in any way she could see, but one of the bodyguards pulled out a cellphone.

He even had people to make his phone calls for him? Did she want to know who was getting that call?

Not really.

She'd practically had Ruth and Dan up her grill for days and when she could really use them? Where were they?

It was almost magic when they both appeared around the corner of a building.

She blinked, because she could with the glasses hiding her eyes. It was almost a classic good news/bad news moment.

She didn't like being found in St. Cyr's company. It didn't seem like it would help her innocence profile.

But she was glad they were there to be witnesses and hopefully also a buffer.

She had to compress her lips to keep from twitching.

She lifted a hand to get their attention and both bodyguards went into alert position.

She turned her hand. "It's a wave, not a weapon anywhere I know about."

Her hands weren't lethal weapons, nor insured by anyone.

Dan and Ruth changed course and she saw the change in their body language when they realized who she was with.

Why did she want to protest that she wasn't with them?

* * *

Dan had no way to tell what Gemma was thinking or feeling. Her body language was relaxed and her eyes were hidden behind her big, Audrey Hepburn sunglasses.

He didn't know what to think, but he knew he felt a lot of things.

Uneasy.

Wary.

Suspicious (of St. Cyr, though it was troubling to find them together).

Worry for Gemma.

Probably some other stuff he didn't have time to figure out.

"They are here to see Raymond Blaine," Gemma said when they came up beside her.

St. Cyr's gaze moved between them. Would he recognize a Baker, Dan wondered? He ought to. He'd had dealings with enough of us. And Dan knew he and his brothers shared some of the family features.

Dan pulled out his ID and showed it to St. Cyr. "CGIS," he said. "This is Agent Fossette."

St. Cyr didn't stiffen. He'd had too much experience with law enforcement to make predictable moves. Or moves of any kind.

"CGIS?" One of the bodyguards asked.

"Coast Guard Investigative Service."

"Never heard of it," the other bodyguard said.

This was not unexpected, even for a bad guy.

"No reason you should have," Ruth said, "is there?"

The bodyguard looked uncertain for a moment and said slowly, "No."

It sounded more like a "yes."

Dan glanced around, wondering why they were all out here—oh, right. She wouldn't want them onboard. Abbot must be gone because he wouldn't have left her out here on her own.

"Miss Hammond, we've been trying to reach you," Ruth said.

"Is Ray really," her voice broke a little too perfectly, "dead?" She lifted a hand to cover her mouth. The lipstick on her lips was like a splash of blood in the light from the sun.

"I'm afraid so," Dan said. "We understand that you went to New Orleans?"

"No offense," her head moved in Gemma's direction, "but I needed to get ground under my feet. I've only just got my land legs back."

Miss Hammond shifted on the seat, then regretted it, if her jerk was any indication.

"Can't we find a better place to do this?" she asked, extending a hand so that Dan had to pull her to her feet. Her smile was automatically sweet, like a habit she couldn't break. "Thank you."

"We'll need to question all of you," Ruth said. "We can go to the Coast Guard station—"

"I'm staying here," St. Cyr said with cool indifference.

Dan glanced at the sun then back at the wise guy.

Ruth turned to Gemma. "Is it all right if Miss Hammond and I go on board? It shouldn't take long."

"Of course." She turned with them. "I'll just go…" She pointed at the *Reel Escape*.

Did St. Cyr shift a little? By the time Dan looked at him, he'd stopped. His lips were pursed.

"When I'm done with Mr. St. Cyr," Dan said, "I'll come find you, if I may?"

"Of course," she said again, following the two women. She and Ruth had to help Miss Hammond to board.

Dan turned back, finding that being out in the public, in plain view of God and everyone, didn't help that much. It was still three-to-one.

"Baker," St. Cyr said. "Any relation..."

"Yes," Dan said. "Can you account for your movements for the last couple of days? Say, from when you left the *Reel Escape* to now?"

St. Cyr lifted a hand.

"Mr. St. Cyr was driven back to New Orleans. He has been at home until we drove down here with him today," the bodyguard on the right said.

And Dan was sure they'd be happy to testify to that, whether it was true or not.

"How did you happen to be traveling with Miss Hammond?"

There was a long, really long pause. None of the men looked at each other. And St. Cyr didn't signal anyone to talk for him. Dan resisted the urge to say, "Anyone?"

His silence finally drew a reluctant response from St. Cyr.

"She'd given me her cellphone number, so when I knew I was coming down, I called her to see if she needed a ride."

Dan lifted his brows. "How did you know she was in New Orleans. You left before she did."

Another long pause ensued.

"Raymond told me," St. Cyr finally said.

And no one could ask him for corroboration.

"How did Raymond die?" St. Cyr asked. "Miss Bailey said it was an accident?"

"Cause of death is still being determined," Dan said. "Was he doing legal work for you?"

St. Cyr blinked. "We discussed several topics of concern."

I'm sure you did.

"Mr. Blaine indicated to us that you were thinking of investing in his reality show."

"Did he."

It wasn't a question. Dan was pretty much feeling his way here. He wished his brother, Frank, were here, but then he'd have to confess what he was really doing. But it would have helped to have a pro here right now.

Dan pulled out the two photos of Perkins and held them out. One of the bodyguards took them from him and held them so St. Cyr could see.

"Ever seen him?"

"No."

"His name is Perkins. Henry Perkins."

"It's a very common name."

"It is," Dan agreed. "Met one recently?"

"No."

His lawyer had taught him well. Only answer the question you've been asked. Don't elaborate ever.

Dan took the photos back, but then, on impulse asked if either of the two bodyguards had ever seen him.

Of course, they said no. Even if St. Cyr hadn't been there, they wouldn't have admitted anything.

"Who is he?" One of them asked.

"His body was found not far from where Blaine's body turned up," Dan said, hoping the information share was the right move.

The flicker of St. Cyr's lashes was more telling than a blink, in Dan's opinion. The information had struck a nerve, he just wished he knew which nerve.

"Blaine," St. Cyr said, "had some proprietary information, covered by client privilege. I would like to have it."

"You'll need to be more specific," Dan said.

"It was a computer file."

"I'll see what I can find out," Dan said. Hadn't Gemma said

Ashley Hammond had taken his laptop? No, she'd thought she had. All Hammond had today was a handbag. "Thank you for your help."

He managed to say it without a trace of irony. St. Cyr may have moved his head in a nod. Or not. Dan wasn't sure.

"If we have more questions, I assume you have no objection to us contacting you?"

"You can contact me," St. Cyr said.

Dan noticed he didn't agree to answer any questions or indicate he didn't object. Neither was a huge surprise.

He hadn't liked admitting he wanted a file. Interesting that he'd wanted it bad enough to make the drive all the way down here.

Dulac was the last stop before the Gulf of Mexico, at least on this peninsula.

Dan turned and headed toward the *Reel Escape*. It wasn't easy to turn his back on those three, but he managed it without dying.

He jumped aboard. There was no sign of the women, but there was a murmur of voices to follow. Just before he ducked his head to change decks, he looked back.

St. Cyr was still sitting there in the high hot sun.

chapter nine

Gemma looked up from the map she'd been studying as Dan came up the lower deck stairs.

"Is he gone?"

Dan shook his head. "Not yet."

"Weird."

He couldn't argue with that. "You said that Ashley took Blaine's laptop?"

She frowned, trying to remember exactly what she knew. "He said she was going to New Orleans to work on the footage."

"So you didn't see the laptop?"

Gemma shook her head. "Little Abner and Fred helped her carry a couple of bags down. I was changing the sheets." She hesitated. "Is it important?"

"All she has is a handbag today," Dan pointed out.

"Well, if she came down here with creepy dude, she could have left her stuff in his limo." She considered him for several seconds. "Your people searched here."

"Blaine wouldn't have been able to hide anything anywhere here? Without your knowing it?"

"Hide what?" It was need to know. "I don't think he could hide a laptop."

"What if it was just a computer file?"

107

Gemma laughed. "He could hide that online. Or it might have been on his phone."

"We haven't found his phone."

Gemma wasn't surprised. Losing stuff in the swamp must be dead easy. She gave a mental wince at the thought.

"St. Cyr seemed to think it was something physical."

Gemma chuckled. "And he's like a thousand years old."

Dan grinned. "Now I feel like I am, too."

Gemma propped a hip against a console. "How long have you been an agent?" She had the distinct feeling it hadn't been that long, though she wasn't sure why.

"About a year," he admitted. "I was in search and rescue until Ruth recruited me."

That was interesting. "That's kind of a big change."

"Well, yes and no," Dan looked wry. "Cops run in my family. We've had to branch out a bit into other branches so the NOPD didn't get too crowded with Bakers."

She almost frowned. How many of them were there?

"I went into the Coast Guard, well," he rubbed his face, "as a protest I guess."

"That's quite the rebellion there." On one level she was aware they were talking like people, not agent and suspect and that she liked it, but she didn't let the thought move into her head. She was enjoying the moment too much to let thinking mess it up.

Dan laughed. "Yeah."

"So what made you decide to make the leap?"

"I broke my leg during a rescue and realized I was getting old —not quite a thousand years yet—and I called Ruth."

"And here you are." She didn't realize she was smiling at first. It was the way his face changed that clued her in.

"Here I am."

"How did your family feel about the change?" Her gaze felt like his had hooked hers, in some weird way. It was as if they were having this normal, get-to-know-you exchange but at this other level, something else was happening.

Dan rubbed his face again, but he did it without breaking eye contact.

"You haven't told them." She leaned back, her smile widening. "For a year."

"You have to understand, I come from a big family. That's a lot of people telling you they told you so."

"I can't imagine," Gemma said. She really couldn't imagine. She'd only had one "I told you so" person in her life, Little Abner. Fish hadn't been the type.

Behind him, she heard the sliding door going back. They both stiffened at the same time, the intimacy of the moment evaporating. But the warmth of it lingered.

* * *

Dan was sorry for the interruption as Gemma retreated behind her careful facade once more.

He'd enjoyed the light exchange, though he'd exchanged more information than she had. He didn't regret it, which was kind of a surprise.

As Ruth and Miss Hammond entered, he felt that image of the tangled and knotted tree roots come back to him, this time with a stronger sense that what he couldn't see would make better sense of what he did see.

But the roots felt as if they'd taken a sudden dip underground, so he struggled to trace the connections, let alone trace anything back to its source.

Ashley Hammond looked sulky and immediately dropped into a chair, crossing her arms over her chest.

Dan arched an inquiring brow in Ruth's direction.

"According to Miss Hammond, Blaine didn't have a laptop with him. He did everything on his phone. But he also had one of those devices that let you use GPS to stay in contact."

Dan straightened. "Our people..."

"I told them to start looking," Ruth interrupted.

For the first time, it felt like they might catch a break.

The *Reel Escape* moved as someone came aboard. Footsteps approached and then Little Abner appeared in the hatch.

The scowl faded as his gaze found Ruth.

Dan straightened a little. Had the old rascal taken a shine to Ruth? He looked away to get the grin under control and his gaze intersected with Gemma's.

Her lips were also twitching and he felt the connection reform between them.

"I seriously don't want to be here," Miss Hammond said, her tone on the shrill side.

Dan turned to find her looking at him, then at Gemma as if she couldn't quite believe what she saw. What had she seen?

He resisted the urge to tug at the neck of his shirt. He hadn't done anything.

"And yet you came down here with St. Cyr," Ruth pointed out.

"That was not—" She cut off the sentence.

What had she been about to say. That it wasn't her choice to come down here?

"If St. Cyr threatened you in any way," Ruth began.

Miss Hammond gave a brittle laugh. "Of course not. Is there somewhere I could hire a car? I don't want to hang around here if Ray…"

Her voice trailed off. Either because she realized how callous she sounded or perhaps she realized there was nowhere to rent a car in Cocodrie.

"We are told that Mr. Blaine's father is on the way," Dan said. "Maybe he'll give you a lift back to New Orleans, though his business here will probably take time, too."

"Or you might be able to hitch a ride on a boat heading up to Chauvin," Ruth said. "There might be a place to rent a car there."

She sounded doubtful.

Miss Hammond closed her eyes and moaned.

Dan couldn't find it in him to blame her. She was well and truly stuck.

"Are you going to want your stateroom back?" Gemma asked without enthusiasm.

Miss Hammond looked up. "I guess for now. My luggage is in Claude's limo." She brightened a little. "Ray's room is available now, isn't it?"

"It's a crime scene," Ruth said.

"I'll see if one of St. Cyr's people can bring your luggage here," Gemma said.

"I'll do it," Dan said. He couldn't explain how much he didn't like her even talking to the man. And her smile was grateful. It was nice to know she didn't like talking to him.

* * *

"I'll go get your room ready," Gemma said, hoping she'd managed to hide her total lack of enthusiasm from Ashley. Technically they owed her at least one, maybe two days aboard. She was starting to lose track of the days, or they were just blurring together. Whichever, it wasn't like her.

As she left the flybridge, she heard Little Abner ask, "Are you sure we have to stay out of Blaine's stateroom?"

She didn't hear Ruth's response, but when she got below the yellow crime scene tape across the door was like an exclamation point on the end of her "yes, I'm sure."

It didn't take her long to change the bed and wipe down the bathroom, but she'd need to do some laundry before she could change the bed again.

She stopped, doing some mental math. At least she had a couple more days worth of underwear.

When the room was ready, she didn't go up right away. She sat in the room's lone chair and tried to figure out what she felt. She finally found the right word.

Crowded.

She felt crowded on every side.

St. Cyr outside.

Her bio-father incoming. She hadn't been ready to hear that.

Ashley and her whining.

Ruth and Dan? They'd been up in her grill for several days, but she didn't mind them. Even if they did think she was a murderer, she liked them.

Her instincts about people were usually right. She considered the thought. Actually, so far they'd always been right. Maybe not always bullseye right, but on target.

She heard movement out in the corridor and got up. Dan appeared, carrying Ashley's two cases.

She smiled because he'd kept a St. Cyr goon from coming aboard.

"Thank you," she said.

He set them down with a grin. He seemed to know what she meant because he said, "Be a pity to mess the room up again."

She chuckled. "Or creeped up."

It was his turn to chuckle. She liked the trickle of warmth that slid through her, even if she was still flushed from wrestling with the bedding.

Dan sobered and her insides tensed.

"Are you really okay? You've had a crap tone of stuff hit and very little time to deal with it."

The warmth got somehow sweeter. Maybe he didn't think she was a murderer.

She met his gaze, letting her defenses ease. "I have no idea."

She was definitely in a state of unfamiliar flux. Had she ever felt this way before? Once, she decided, when Seth had offered her a job.

"What do you really do?" Dan asked, his tone quiet and non-threatening.

She was acutely aware she didn't want to lie to him.

"I'm not a spy or an agent," she said. It was true she was an operative for Enigma, but she didn't spy on people.

"But you're not a secretary."

"No." She sighed, trying to find the right word for what she did without giving too much away. She had a feeling though, or she hoped she had a feeling that this wouldn't make it into the official file. But even if it did, she trusted Dan more than Seth.

It might have been a blinding revelation moment.

"I compile information," she finally said.

"Information?" Dan looked and sounded surprised. "What kind of information?"

"All kinds." She bit her lip, because she was getting close to disclosing something she'd agreed not to in her non-disclosure agreement.

"WHART," he said.

Gemma didn't blink. She didn't even wonder how he'd found out. She hadn't been as paranoid about getting her picture taken five years ago.

"I like knowing things," she admitted. "I thought about becoming a park ranger."

"Why didn't you?"

Money, she could have told him. When Seth appeared with his job offer, she'd been trying to figure out how to fund the rest of her degree. But it was more than that.

"Too limiting," she said. "I like to know a lot of things." And she was good at finding out lots of things.

Dan looked at her with questions in his eyes, but there was something more, something that bumped up that sweet warmth that had gathered around her heart.

"You're an enigma," he said.

She couldn't help the jerk and his brows arched

"Did I say something wrong?"

She shook her head. "No, you didn't say anything wrong."

The atmosphere between them changed as the questions faded from his gaze and was replaced by something that was…nice.

"I like you, Gemma," he said, his tone just a bit surprised.

By the words or the feeling?

"I like you, too." It was the truth. She did. She probably liked him more than he liked her, but that was okay. She was the "just a friend," not the romantic lead in the production of her life. She did have an uneasy awareness that her liking for Dan went beyond her own normal.

She carefully directed her thoughts back into safer paths as Dan took a step toward her.

The room was small, so this upped the proximity factor a lot.

Gemma tipped her head back. She was hoping and she knew it.

He seemed to know it, too. His head bent and their lips touched. Briefly, mostly just a brush because they were about to be interrupted.

She sighed. She thought he did, too, as he stepped back just in time.

Ruth peered in. "She's wondering if her room is ready?"

Ruth did not sound happy about being Ashley's messenger.

"It's ready," Gemma said, giving Ruth a look of fellow feeling. "I'll go tell her."

chapter ten

Dan twitched his lips, trying to erase the lingering traces of the all too brief contact. He didn't dare look at himself in a mirror for fear of seeing the same look in his eyes, that he'd seen in his brothers just before they went down.

He wasn't sure why they all seemed to be romance-averse. His dad, Zach, had been happily married three times now. At least number three held no risk of adding to Zach's Baker's dozen. He'd chosen an old high school friend, not a late life crisis bride.

Unlike some of his siblings, he hadn't been singed by love. He'd just been too busy, or maybe he'd kept himself too busy to settle down. It was possible they all had a fear, not of commitment but of children.

He still couldn't believe Alex, the eldest of them, had not only married again, but had an actual kid. Both of these were on his list of "would never happen."

And then there was the "shouldn't have happened" part. Was the kiss an ethical breach or just poor judgement? He considered the question and decided it edged over into poor judgement—that didn't feel like it.

His gut said she was a good person. He considered this. So far, his gut hadn't let him down. It wasn't that he was always right, no way no how. It was just that when it counted, when he was in the maze, he counted on his gut.

He felt reasonably clear, though he shouldn't do it again no matter how much he wanted to. And he had no intention of telling Ruth about his possible lapse.

He made his way back up top, following Ruth and Gemma. Despite his best efforts to detach from the moment, his gaze kept seeking out Gemma. Why?

She was thin, not painfully so, just thin and kind of wiry. She moved easily around the Hatteras. From what he'd read, she'd been mostly raised on it. She'd attended school from time to time, but was mostly home—or boat schooled.

She passed a GED exam and had gone to university until something had happened. She hadn't flunked out, they knew that. Her grades had been exceptional during that short time in public education.

He already knew she was smart. Now he knew she was good at finding out things. Had she turned this skill on their investigation?

He wanted to be annoyed at the thought, but mostly he wished he could have her look at their autopsy results—from her WHART perspective. If the kills had been a wild animal…

He sighed, not sure what that would change, except maybe bring a bunch of Rougarou hunters down on them.

They were waiting for DNA test results taken from all three victims to rule out—or in—a predator. They were sure it hadn't been an alligator.

They also needed the toxology results. Their medical examiner suspected they'd been drugged, though if it had been any of the so-called date rape drugs, they might not show up in a drug screen.

On a sudden impulse, he grabbed Ruth's arm before she could follow Gemma back into the salon.

"I'd like to have Gemma take a look at the autopsy reports."

Actual expression broke out on her face. "You're not serious?"

"She's been to WHART training," Ruth's face changed to confused, so he explained, "Wildlife-Human Attack Response Training."

If she'd done that five years ago, he'd bet she'd taken other types of animal attack training, too, though he was sure there wasn't Rougarou-specific training. "You don't think she killed our victims anymore than I do."

She gave a sigh. "No, but I don't have the same certainty about Abner Abbot."

Dan grinned. "That's just because he's flirting with you, or at least trying to."

Ruth looked amused instead of annoyed. "He's a character."

"Well?" Dan watched her and knew the moment he'd won. He might have felt a stab of guilt about not telling her about the other things Gemma had said, but they really hadn't had time for a debrief.

It felt a bit like they were riding the surface of swamp slime and just barely keeping their balance.

He did not want to fall in.

"Fine." She gave him an annoyed look when he grinned. "It might help us find out something about her."

He'd take what he could get.

Inside the salon, they found that Gemma had gone out onto the deck. She'd taken time to don her big shady hat and almost as big sunglasses. Her clothes covered her from her neck to her wrists and down to her ankles. Her deck shoes kept the sun off her feet.

How did she manage to look cool and almost surreal leaning against the railing, her attention seemingly focused on something far away?

"Gemma," he spoke her name, aware he should be calling her Miss Bailey. Was there a song about a woman with that name? It didn't feel like it quite fit, but found himself thinking the tune and the words, "won't you come home."

Bill Bailey. That was it. Well, it was close. He stopped his thoughts there as she turned around.

"I thought maybe you'd left," she said. Her tone was cool, but a slight smile lingered around the edges of her mouth, as if her thoughts had been happy ones.

"Do you want us to leave?" Ruth asked.

He couldn't tell if the question surprised her. The glasses hid a lot of her face and all of her eyes.

"No." Her shoulders moved in a quick and graceful shrug.

She didn't elaborate, but Dan had a feeling it had to do with St. Cyr. He could see him still sitting on the bench, though someone had brought him an umbrella. Dan's lips twitched. They must have had to purchase it locally. It was a vibrant purple, with a black frill around the edges.

They were most commonly carried during processions, but they had to be desperate out there.

The bodyguards each had one, too.

It had to be brutal out there.

He thought about his approach, even wondering if Ruth would jump in if he didn't. But he felt like a somewhat sideways approach might be better. Especially after the kiss. Fortunately, it was so hot, he was sure no one would notice the warming of his cheeks.

"Gemma," he half turned to bring Ruth into the conversation, "was telling me that she is good at finding out things."

Ruth didn't give him a look. He had a feeling she wanted to, though.

"Is there anything you've found out that we might need to know?" Ruth asked.

Gemma leaned back against the railing, her hands supporting her on each side. "Are you afraid I'm going to turn into the annoying amateur sleuth? Because I don't mix fiction into my reality."

"Actually we were kind of hoping you might be the inspired

amateur." Dan pulled out his cellphone and navigated to the autopsy results he'd been sent.

"Amateur I can do," she said, but she sounded intrigued.

"I, we," he corrected, "were wondering if you'd be willing to look at the autopsy results of our three victims." He found himself looking at one of the photographs and grimaced. "Feel free to say no. They are pretty gruesome."

She pulled her sunglasses off and now he could see she definitely was intrigued. She held out a hand for his cellphone. He didn't hesitate, though he did wonder if he should have. He eased his unease by standing by her side, so he could see over her shoulder.

She took her time, both in reading the medical examiner's findings and studying the photographs. She zoomed in on certain spots, then backed out to zoom in on a different spot.

At some point, Ruth sat down. Dan wished he could, too. Gemma appeared totally engrossed.

Finally, she seemed to return to the present. She looked up.

"Your medical examiner did a good job. He or she..." she hesitated.

"She," Ruth said.

"She did a good job. I agree an animal didn't attack any of them. Any critter damage was definitely postmortem. Ledet has the least of that damage because you found him so quickly."

"So not the Rougarou?" Ruth asked dryly.

"I think they tried hard to make it look an animal attack," Gemma said. "But the slashes are the same on all three victims, except..."

She stopped and navigated to one of the photographs from the autopsy.

"See this slash? It's on his back and it breaks the pattern. All three victims have an out-of-pattern slash, just in different places."

"What do you think it means?" Ruth came over to join them.

"Well, I have a nasty suspicious mind, but I'll bet they were darted and they tried to cover it up with the slashes. If your medical examiner hasn't already looked there, I'd suggest she see if she can find some sub-dermal damage. The slashes appear superficial, but it's hard to tell for sure from a photograph."

Ruth had already pulled out her cell and was typing a text.

"But why?" Dan asked. "If it were someone besides Blaine, I'd suspect he was trying to create some media hype for his show. But he's one of our victims."

"Blaine might not be the only one trying to create hype—or an aura of danger to keep people away," she said thoughtfully.

"A kind of warn-off," Dan said slowly. Could there really be something valuable out there?

"You do have one to three people who disappeared a long time ago," Gemma said.

"And one of them is dead." Dan lifted his gaze from the cell and the gruesome image there, to meet Gemma's gaze. He might be impressed by how clinical she looked—and sounded. "Is this what you do?"

The question surprised them both.

"I told you what I do," she said. "I find out things."

"What kind of things?" Ruth asked.

"Things that are need to know." Her gaze turned assessing as she studied Ruth and then turned to Dan.

The clean light scent of her lightened the heavy humid air.

"Non-disclosure agreement?" Ruth sounded like a light bulb was going off.

Gemma gave a shrug that might have been agreement, but her eyes said yes. So it was so non-disclosure she couldn't even talk about it?

Ruth nodded as if satisfied. "As an *inspired* amateur," she said, "who do you think are suspects?"

Gemma handed him his phone and sat on the end of a recliner. "Well, the other two people who disappeared, for starters. Blaine would have been, but we'll never know if he knew or wandered into the wrong place at the wrong time." She paused, tapping her chin reflectively. "I'm inclined toward him knowing. There's St. Cyr who..." She made an expressive grimace.

"Yeah," Dan threw a look in St. Cyr's direction. He seemed to be picnicking out there. A cloth had been spread on the bench, and another man holding an umbrella had appeared. So they had bright green, purple, bright blue, and yellow now.

They were almost a procession. His grin faded. A funeral procession. All they needed was the brass band.

"He's still there." Gemma sighed. "Why is he hanging around here?"

"The computer file?" Ruth suggested.

"He'd be better off trying to find Blaine's cellphone or his GPS device," Gemma said.

"He's waiting for something." Dan thought about it. "Or someone."

* * *

Could St. Cyr be waiting for Little Abner? Gemma resisted the impulse to chew on her lower lip. Seth discouraged anything that could be a giveaway.

The unease she'd felt increased with the rising temperatures. How hot was it, anyway? She wanted to pull out her cellphone and look, but that could also be a giveaway.

She almost did a wry smile giveaway because she wasn't sure what she'd be giving away by doing anything.

The impulse to hide what she felt could be reaching a weird extreme.

And then, because she really didn't want to think about it with Dan and Ruth there, the kiss came back to her. Was it a kiss? It had been so brief, but so startlingly sweet. She resisted the impulse to run her finger along her lower lip. That *was* a giveaway, and she knew why she didn't want to give that away.

But she'd sure have liked more, or at least longer. She'd just had time to process the touch and inhale his yummy scent—

which was kind of amazing given the temperature, not to mention the humidity.

So little to make her feel dizzy even now.

For all she knew, Dan kissed like that all the time.

No. He didn't. He was careful even with his casual contact. He was a nice guy. She felt the certainty of this in her gut and it rarely let her down.

So, knowing that, what did it all mean?

And why was she thinking romance novel thoughts when a wise guy was picnicking just across the way.

And her biological parent was incoming.

Maybe. He might not be coming here. It's not like he'd tried to see her in the past thirty-five years. He could just be coming to get his son's body and demand action from the authorities. That's what influential people did in shows. Or…

He could be the *who* that St. Cyr was waiting for.

She considered this and gave it a tentative not likely.

St. Cyr wasn't the type to sit in the hot sun on the off chance that someone would show up.

And then the weirdest thought of all came to her.

What if he was waiting for Ruth and Dan to leave so he could see *her?*

She explored that thought, but she could only think of two reasons why he might want to talk to her.

He knew who her biological father was and for reasons not currently obvious that mattered to the wise guy. Or…

He knew who she worked for. She supposed it was possible. Not even Seth was perfect, though she wouldn't even think that in his presence.

Okay, she added one more. What if he thought she knew where the whatever he was looking for was?

That sentence kind of made her head hurt. At least she hadn't said it out loud.

"I have an idea," Dan said.

Gemma didn't mind getting pulled from her painful and not

Pirogue Wipeout

grammatically correct thoughts.

He gave Ruth a wary glance, like he wasn't sure she'd like the idea.

"We both leave…"

Gemma felt a jolt of surprise. Retreat didn't seem to go with their personas. They'd struck her as full steam ahead types.

"And then I can get a lift back here, board on the aft side, out of sight."

"And what am I supposed to do?" Ruth asked. She didn't sound super thrilled at Dan wanting the action hero role.

Gemma kind of liked the idea. She'd like to see him flex his muscles and kick some tush. He could take the bodyguards and she take down St. Cyr. The sad part? That scenario probably wouldn't lead to an actual, sustained kiss.

"You could try to track down the GPS," Gemma suggested, wishing she had access to the data to see for herself.

"I have people for that," Ruth said.

Gemma's lips twitched.

"You could get us some backup," Dan pointed out.

"There is that." Ruth still hesitated. "How fast can you get back here?"

St Cyr did have to be tired of sitting in the sun.

"You watch out of sight while I get around?" Dan added, "And I'll hurry."

Ruth looked at Gemma. "Are you okay with this? It leaves you hung out to dry for a bit."

Gemma appeared to consider the proposal. It wouldn't do to look too eager to be staked out like a lamb.

She wasn't, but they didn't know that. Finally she nodded.

"If you stay in sight, you should be all right," Ruth said.

Now that he'd got his way, Dan didn't look eager to leave.

"I'll be all right," she told them. She produced an "I'm being brave" look for them.

Dan touched her arm. "I'll be back as quick as I can."

"I know." She did. He was a good guy.

123

She stood at the railing watching them walk out of sight without looking in St. Cyr's direction.

She strolled away from the rail, and once out of sight, did a fast walk to her cabin.

She pulled her handgun out from under her mattress and checked the chambers. Her tactical holster was also under the mattress with some extra magazines.

She strapped it around her waist, holstered her weapon so it was snug in the curve of her back, and then added the extra magazines to their handy slots.

She did some rearranging of her clothes so she could get quick access to her weapon and then studied what she could see in the bathroom mirror.

She didn't think they'd search her, but she strapped a knife to her calf just above the inside of her ankle. It always good to be prepared.

She checked the security camera with her phone and saw that St. Cyr and his goons were on the move.

She made her way back to the main deck, watching their approach from the shadows.

They'd probably ask for her phone, so she set all the cameras and recording equipment to voice and motion activated. She installed them to protect them from random pirates when they were out in the Gulf.

Then she headed up to the flybridge and went out onto the deck. She picked a chair that would give the camera a good view of the intruders but also turned their attention away from the canal side.

She settled back to wait.

It didn't take long for the three men to find her. She could hear a third man searching below decks. St. Cyr's driver? A third bodyguard?

The ratio of bad guys to them was still doable, she decided.

She heard a raised, very female voice carry up through the

decks. She switched to that camera in time to see Ashley slam her door.

She'd forgotten she was there. That wasn't like her, but she'd had a lot on her mind.

It was the driver who took up a position outside her door. At least, she'd been alive when the door closed. The other two bodyguards made brief appearances in the cameras as they searched below decks.

Where was St. Cyr?

She didn't frown. Oh, those giveaways. Sometimes she missed them.

She rotated through the camera views until she found him. He was waiting outside the flybridge for his backup.

When they joined him, she shut down her phone and rose, getting her balance, and easing her body into a fast response position. None of the three men appeared to notice.

It was funny how people didn't notice what they weren't expecting. There was a long list of people who had underestimated her, but they weren't here to warn them.

The bodyguards hands hung loosely by their sides, but probably close to their weapons as they followed St. Cyr out onto the sunny side of the deck.

That was kind of a bonus. Their faces were still red from their prolonged picnic.

She couldn't think of a reason for them to kill her. That didn't mean they didn't have one.

They might just be here to intimidate her, but why? Even the connection she'd found with Blaine and the St. Cyrs didn't explain this move.

At least, it was possible he thought she knew something. That covered a lot of ground.

She stowed the questions with no answers. It was pointless. St. Cyr would either tell her or he wouldn't.

She knew her hat shaded her face, and her sunglasses were

almost as big as potholes. Should she remove them? While she debated this, she spoke.

"I don't remember inviting any of you on board."

"I want to talk to you," St. Cyr said.

She considered how hostile to get. These were very bad people.

"I had that impression earlier." She hesitated, then removed the sunglasses and tossed them onto the chair. If she had to move fast, they'd come off anyway.

"We were interrupted."

Not a moment too soon.

"Yes." She moved over the dockside rail and leaned against it, her elbows on the rail. This put her hands close to her gun, and it forced them to turn toward her and away from the canal.

She'd never actually shot anyone, but Seth had made sure she could. She marked their new positions.

One of the bodyguards did glance behind from time to time, but there was a lot of traffic out there.

Witnesses, lots of witnesses. At least that is what she hoped they'd see.

St. Cyr regarded her without speaking. In his dark suit that emphasized his gray skin he was truly the specter at the feast.

And the people on the boats going by would notice how out of place he looked. His bodyguards, too. She studied the three and had to restrain a smile.

They looked like a scene from a Bruce Willis movie.

The silence built, but Gemma didn't mind. Time was on her side. More people would see them, both out on the canal and around the marina.

And they'd all probably watched St. Cyr and his goons come aboard.

Gemma didn't offer St. Cyr a seat or invite him to speak. He glanced at the deck offerings and picked a chair, seating himself as dubiously as he had on the bench.

The bodyguards didn't move with him. They didn't think she

was the threat here. That was interesting. Were they expecting someone else? Little Abner or Dan?

"Blaine." St. Cyr dropped the name into the silence.

It didn't give her much to go on, since there were two of them.

He shifted and she gathered he wasn't used to having to ask for anything.

"Did he tell you why he came here?"

"To film the Rougarou."

He made an impatient movement, then lifted a hand to his bodyguards, both of whom had shifted at his movement.

"You surely didn't believe that?" The cool voice warmed slightly with scorn.

"It wasn't my job to believe or disbelieve. We were hired to get him from point A to point B." Two sentences in a row would have caused Seth to raise his sculpted eyebrows almost to his perfect hairline.

But it was hot.

St. Cyr glanced around as if he expected someone to suddenly appear. Or as if the boat hadn't already been searched.

"Your partner not here?"

Gemma considered her answer. He had to know Little Abner wasn't here, so what did he really want to know?

She opted for a shrug that could have meant anything.

She sensed a stalemate. He didn't want to give her information. He wanted to get it.

She didn't want to give information. She wasn't sure she wanted to get any.

It was common ground in a weird way, but not something that would forward their interaction.

St. Cyr's hands clenched his thin knees and he looked down.

He must be feeling the heat more than she was in that suit. She'd have felt sorry for him if he weren't so profoundly creepy.

She'd melt into a puddle on the deck before she made anything easy for him—all without looking like that is what she was doing.

She knew her gaze gave nothing away. Shadow was completely online.

"If this vessel were moving," St. Cyr began, then paused.

"We don't have permission to move," she said.

"Surely the Coast Guard knows…" he stopped again, perhaps realizing he might be about to give something away.

"The harbor master doesn't care either way. There are procedures we are required to follow."

Unexpectedly one of the bodyguards spoke.

"You can't just set sail when you want to?"

"There are security checks, we'd need to plot a course, and then file it with the harbor master, and then he'd have to clear us to depart."

"Interesting," the man said, then looked almost discomfited when St. Cyr and the other bodyguard gave him looks. "Sorry."

St. Cyr turned back to Gemma. "Could we go inside?"

Gemma pursed her lips, letting some regret appear. "Sorry, no."

St. Cyr almost looked startled. She figured she knew why. Thing to do was to not explain, to not give a why or why not. That way no one could try to "help" you with your problem of not wanting to do what they asked. It left them nowhere to go.

Well, it left most people no where to go. This was a wise guy. He might be able to find a way.

His expression had shut, and she sensed he was calculating the odds of using threats. Once he did, there was no going back to this "friendly" exchange.

They might could force her inside without people noticing, but he'd drawn attention to himself with his weird picnic and the umbrellas. People would remember him.

They'd remember him coming aboard.

He might be able to intimidate them into silence, but he couldn't intimidate Ruth or Dan.

They didn't know that, of course.

Which was probably why St. Cyr was currently calculating the pros and cons of escalating.

Because of all the traffic going by, the boat rocked persistently, if not consistently. Still, she felt the shift of something interrupting a wave. Was it Dan?

She wished she could check the cameras. But she didn't bring her high-tech gear on vacation.

She may have imagined the oh-so-slight relaxing of his aspect.

"My mother knew your mother," he said, "only slightly, of course. They didn't occupy the same social circles."

Gemma managed to control everything but a flicker of her lashes. Which mother was he talking about?

"They never proved anything against her," he went on in his cold, relentless tone. "She, my mother, said you look a lot like her."

She didn't ask how his mother had gotten a look at her. She wasn't stupid—she hoped. She couldn't see the whole of it yet, but this felt like the landmine Fish had tried to keep her from stepping on.

She tried out several responses inside her head, but she didn't like any of them. He was jabbing in the dark. No reason to give him even a thread of light to follow.

She tipped her head and looked interested. It was one of several expressions she used when she was feeling her way through a situation.

Situation.

She could have laughed at herself for using such a downplaying word. She'd caught it from Seth, of course. Everything was a situation to him, even if shooting happened. Or so she'd heard.

She'd never been in a shooting situation. Was she in one now?

The sound of canal traffic blurred all sound, so she wasn't sure about the splash. Neither bodyguard reacted. Was it, could it be Dan? And did she want him to hear this?

"When she disappeared, according to my mother," St. Cyr

said, "they all wondered, of course." He paused. "But no one really believed she'd died."

He was giving up tidbits of information in hopes of shocking her into giving up something. And it almost worked.

She was pregnant. Of course she disappeared.

Thankfully, she didn't say it.

"My mother is dead," she said, opening her eyes so St. Cyr could see how innocently she believed it.

"The name on your birth certificate?" Scorn laced his tone, actual scorn. Was he losing his cool? "That's not your mother."

"My father—"

"Fish Bailey was not your father. He was your uncle."

"How could you know that? Why should I believe *you*?" She didn't emphasis the last word. She didn't have to.

His gaze jumped to hers.

"My source is impeccable."

She waited, holding his gaze even though it felt like spiders crawling down her spine.

"Why?"

"Why what?"

"What," she adjusted her tack slightly, "does it have to do with you?" She resisted the urge to add more to this. *Less is always better.* The world according to Seth.

For the first time, St. Cyr might have been disconcerted. She wasn't sure, but it seemed to her that his face went more blank, possibly even somewhat slack.

They were getting down to it. The landmine was right there. She could almost see it.

chapter eleven

Dan's motorboat lift did a good job getting him close to the *Reel Escape*. Their approach gave him a chance to see the four figures on the upper deck.

Ruth had texted him about three men and St. Cyr boarding. So where was the other guy?

The driver brought the boat alongside without touching the *Reel Escape*. Dan eased up and looked around. There was no one in sight.

He scrambled over the side and gave his driver a thumbs up in thanks before he dropped into a crouch, his head below the gunwale. The *Reel Escape* was in constant motion before the canal traffic. He didn't think his added weight changed that.

He pulled his weapon and waited, his senses on high alert for any change in reaction to his boarding. There were voices drifting down from the upper deck.

He rose and padded quietly around the prow to the dock side, his weapon low so it wouldn't be seen by the people milling around. He stopped to check for that third guy at every porthole. What was he looking for? Then it hit him.

Ashley.

He silently said a word he shouldn't have. Taking extra care, he eased around and looked down the hatchway. There that third guy was, lounging against the wall looking bored. It was the limo driver.

He drew back and realized he could hear snatches of conversation from above.

"…no one really believed…died…" It was the low, cold voice of St. Cyr.

Gemma's voice was clear. "My mother is dead."

"…name…birth certificate…"

Even from here he heard the scorn in St. Cyr's voice.

"…not…mother…"

"My father…"

"Fish Bailey…not…father…uncle…"

Well, this wasn't a newsflash. But he wondered why St. Cyr cared. Even his connection to Blaine didn't explain this move.

"What does it have to do with you?" Gemma's tone wasn't hostile, but it wasn't friendly, as she voiced Dan's question.

He looked up and realized she was leaning against the railing just above him, her elbows propped on the rail.

Good girl. She'd kept them turned away from the canal. Now he wished he knew where they were positioned up there.

He felt the vibration of a text and carefully pulled out his cellphone. It was from Ruth.

Eyes on them. And a picture of the upper deck. Dang, she was good. He wondered where she was, but he'd find out later. He sent a thumbs up and headed down the deck. He needed to get closer.

* * *

Gemma could tell they were reaching the point, though she had no sense of what that point might be.

"Your mother stole something from my family and I want it back."

Gemma blinked. So she'd been right thinking that he thought

Pirogue Wipeout

she knew something. He was wrong, but it felt like his wrong somehow cancelled out her right.

She'd have laughed, but those goons. They didn't look like they had a sense of humor. It was probably written into their contract.

Who was she kidding? Seth would have written it into her contract if he'd thought he could get away with it. Her often inappropriate sense of humor was probably why she was still an operative. That and she didn't want to move up into management. Telling people like her what to do was not her idea of a good time.

Gemma considered a response to St. Cyr, because her random thoughts weren't that helpful. It kind of surprised her when she decided on the truth.

"I never met my mother—that I remember," she added conscientiously. If she was going with the truth, it needed to be almost all the truth. It helped she really didn't know.

"Fish…" began St. Cyr.

"Is dead," she pointed out and thought, *sucks to be you.*

"I'm not a thief," she went on, even though it went against Seth policy. "If I had your something, I'd happily give it back."

She wondered if the sincerity in her voice could reach someone like him.

He studied her for a long moment. "You might not know it is valuable."

"The only thing Fish left to me was half this boat." She hesitated, then decided to go for it. She did not want to be on his hit list. It kind of felt like she'd just gotten out of witness protection and she didn't want to go back in. "If I knew more…"

The silence was as heavy as the humid air.

"It's a wooden figure. About twelve inches high."

Gemma measured the distance with her hands and then shook her head.

"You didn't find anything in his personal effects?"

She shook her head. Fish's personal effects had mostly

consisted of some books and clothing. Oh and some cassette music tapes. Elvis and Waylon Jennings. "Maybe she…sold it?"

Gemma didn't use Mary's name because she wasn't sure she knew it right now. The truth didn't need to be an information dump.

"It has not turned up on the market."

The black market, he didn't say. Had he had it stolen? No, she didn't want to know.

"The reason I ask, is because she gave Fish money before she left. He used it to buy his share of this boat."

It didn't bother her to say this because he knew it already. If he didn't, his "people" weren't worth much.

"Could it have been sold to a private collector?"

"No."

The single word was on the creepy side. He believed it had been handed off to Fish. For the first time, she left the side and went to a chair—one not close to him—and sat down.

Her professional curiosity had been aroused, though it shouldn't be. This was not a client.

"You seem sure," she said. "I need to know what you know. All of it. Unless there are some less than legal parts. I have no desire to hear those."

He'd either tell her or leave. She wasn't sure which she hoped for. Curiosity should not be rearing its head right now.

St. Cyr actually blinked. And for just a moment she saw longing in his eyes. He lowered his lashes and didn't speak.

Gemma sensed movement in the salon behind the three bad guys and let her gaze slid past St. Cyr. It was Dan. She gave a slight, very slight shake. He faded back into the shadows by the curtains.

Gemma waited. She knew how to do this part. She knew her expression was bland and mildly enquiring. She knew exactly how innocuous she looked.

Seth had been known to wonder how she did it. She didn't know. It's not like she'd taken a class on how to be innocuous.

St. Cyr shifted, and she knew he was going to start talking.

"Rougarou," he said. "It's the Rougarou."

* * *

Dan blinked. Their voices were a bit muffled, but he was pretty sure what he'd heard. It's not like it was a word you could mix up with anything else.

He was impressed when Gemma didn't blink.

"The Rougarou." She didn't make it a question, which Dan felt was a good choice. She didn't even sound disbelieving.

"The Rougarou," St. Cyr repeated.

Dan wished he could see St. Cyr's expression right now. He had a feeling the situation could break either way.

"It's a carving of the Rougarou." She opened her mouth to add something, but stopped herself.

If she'd been about to say what he was thinking—that Blaine had probably been looking for that Rougarou, not the real one—it was a good decision.

St. Cyr had just handed her a good motive for killing Blaine.

"That's right." St. Cyr's voice was cool enough to chill the sweat running down Dan's back.

"Why do you think it's here?"

Her question deflected it away from her. It kept things neutral. There was a tone in Gemma's voice that he couldn't quite put a finger on. It was...interesting.

"As you just admitted, Fish and his sister had contact."

"Thirty-five years or so ago." She gave a slight frown that Dan was certain was calculated.

Dan was relieved her tone hadn't changed. She hadn't risen to the bait.

"When did your statue go missing?"

"It was being stored in a warehouse prior to delivery. There was a fire."

That wasn't exactly an answer to her question. He was trying to find out how much she knew.

Don't fall for it.

"Fire and wood doesn't seem like a good combo. You're certain it survived the fire?"

"Other items have appeared." St. Cyr's voice was still cool but unless Dan was fooling himself, the interrogator had become the interrogated.

"Is that why you think she's not dead? Are you sure Fish's sister was the thief?"

"Very."

He'd hired her, Dan thought. That's how he knew.

"Okay, well, the thing is, this is the only physical place Fish ever lived, that I know of. And the Coast Guard just searched us from stem to stern. Was there, could there have been someone else in her life? A partner, perhaps?"

There was a long pause. "There were rumors," St. Cyr admitted.

She leaned forward, resting her elbows on her knees. "It seems odd the statue hasn't turned up. If it's wood, it is possible it didn't survive the fire."

"It did."

He sounded certain, which made Dan frown. Gemma nodded.

"It's a puzzler," Gemma said, with just the right hint of sympathy. "I mean, if you think it's here, you're welcome to search. I just can't see why Fish would hide it and never say anything to anyone about it."

"He could," St. Cyr said, the cold returning to his voice, "have told his partner about it."

"I can see why you'd wonder," Gemma said, "but he had no reason not to tell me when Fish died."

"Unless he planned to keep it for himself. He is in financial difficulties."

Dan mouthed another word he shouldn't.

"Little Abner knows I'd help him if he needed it."

Dan couldn't put his finger on the change in her voice. Her face hadn't changed. Wait, that tingle down his spine was familiar. *Danger.*

Was Gemma Bailey...dangerous?

He heard a cheerful whistle from the direction of the dock. He didn't know why he was certain who it was. Gemma didn't stiffen, but the three men did.

Surely Abbot wasn't going to turn up right now?

"Gemma!" Abbot called out. "You there? Come get some supper with me!"

Dan hesitated, wondering if he should move now, but before he could, he felt the chill of a handgun barrel against the back of his neck.

* * *

Shadow's persona didn't crack, but inside Gemma might have said some words that Fish would have washed her mouth out for even thinking.

She held up a finger to the three men, rose and sauntered over to the rail and looked down.

"Why don't you bring me something?" she suggested. "It's too hot."

Little Abner looked up at her and she knew that somehow, in some way, she'd given herself away. That shouldn't be possible, but he had known her a very long time.

"Tell him to come up," St. Cyr said, the ice in his voice better than a blast of air conditioning.

Gemma hesitated, but it was no use. One of the bodyguards joined her at the railing. Little Abner stared at him. The bodyguard stared back.

"I think I'll come up," Little Abner said.

Was it possible he did have the Rougarou figure? He'd been a little off lately.

"Please sit," St. Cyr said.

Gemma sat. She didn't have much choice. If Little Abner did have it, would it be enough for St. Cyr to get it back?

It might. Still lots of witnesses around. And Dan. Dan was there, hopefully Little Abner wouldn't spot him and get the wrong idea.

The glass doors were shoved open and Dan emerged, followed by St. Cyr's driver, whose gun was pointed at the back of Dan's head. It seemed he'd gotten the right idea about Dan. He signaled for them all to come inside.

She knew how fast a situation could go sideways, but this might be a new record.

***

Dan didn't mention he was a federal agent. St. Cyr knew and didn't care. It was hard to see his end game, though. It wasn't as if Ruth didn't know he was here. And the dock had plenty of foot traffic, with boat traffic on the canal side.

He sensed that St. Cyr wasn't pleased by this turn of events. Maybe his henchman had jumped the gun…literally? The question now? What would he do about it?

St. Cyr might be able to retrieve the situation if he didn't lose his head.

"There's no need for that," Gemma said, nodding at the gun. "If Abner has the figure, he'll give it to you, won't you, Abner?"

Abner looked confused. Dan couldn't tell if it was real or not. He'd had a lot of years to practice on his expressions.

"Figure?"

"Of the Rougarou," Gemma prompted. "Mr. St. Cyr has lost it and wants to find it. Badly."

Did Gemma think Abbot had it? Or was she using the situation to give him information.

"He thinks Fish gave it to you."

"He didn't give me a Rougarou," Abbot said in a scoffing tone. Then he asked, "A Rougarou? Seriously?"

"It's a wooden statue of the Rougarou. Did Fish give you anything? Something he wanted you to keep for him?"

Abbot frowned.

"Around the time he came here with me," Gemma added.

"That was a long time ago," Abbot protested.

"It would be in your best interests to remember," St. Cyr said.

The driver hadn't lowered his gun. The bodyguards hadn't pulled their weapons yet, but their hands were poised to pull.

"If my property is returned to me, we can all forget this minor unpleasantness."

And if Abbot didn't have it? Dan didn't want to think what would happen then.

"He might have left some stuff in a storage hatch, down in the engine space." He gave Gemma an apologetic look. "Forgot all about it. Suspect Fish had forgotten it, too."

That didn't seem likely. Surely St. Cyr wouldn't fall for that?

St. Cyr gave a signal and one of the bodyguards turned, gesturing for Abbot to lead the way.

Okay, St. Cyr had fallen for it. Maybe. Dan didn't lower his guard, though it wasn't much use without a weapon.

"We'll just sit and wait," St. Cyr said, taking a seat and gesturing for them to sit, too.

Dan sat on the couch next to Gemma. What was Abbot hoping for with this move? And before he could corral his thoughts, he did it. He wondered, had her mother been some kind of thief?

He glanced at her. She didn't look concerned. She might have looked bored. Bored like a little kid, he realized.

She crossed her legs. Uncrossed them. Shifted to one side. Then shifted the other way. She looked up, down, and then sighed. Her shifting had made her slump lower on the couch. She put her hands near her tush and pushed up, so that she sat up straight once again.

He'd never once seen her act impatient. Granted they hadn't known each other long, but restlessness had not been visible during any of that time. So what was she up to? Squirming wasn't exactly a plan.

At first, St. Cyr's two goons had looked alert, but now they'd lost interest.

Gemma lifted her heels, one, then the other, repeating it in a tapping sound.

St. Cyr looked at her.

"Sorry," she said. She stopped tapping, but her feet kept moving, as if she couldn't help it.

Her hand was close enough to his thigh, he felt the warmth of it. One of the bodyguards looked at him. He met his gaze calmly, then glanced in the opposite direction from Gemma.

It worked. The bodyguard looked suspiciously in that direction.

"I've never heard of a carving of a Rougarou," Dan said into the silence. They were all listening too hard for sounds from below. Could Abbot actually manage to overpower the younger driver?

"It was carved by a fisherman who saw the creature," St. Cyr said, unexpectedly. "He died not long after and it was considered bad luck to own it."

Dan couldn't help blinking, but then thought, why would a wise guy worry about bad luck? The curse would come up against his bad Karma and make friends.

They heard the sound of footsteps, one pair not as even as when they'd left. All eyes turned toward the doorway.

Dan felt Gemma's hand moving between them. He eased his down next to hers, wondering if she needed the comfort or something. Her hand brushed his and then something cold slid into his hand.

It took all his self-control not to look shocked.

He didn't have much time to do more than clasp the weapon, his thumb finding and releasing the safety as the limo driver staggered through the doorway, with Abbot behind holding his weapon.

Gemma went forward in a somersault that landed her at St. Cyr's feet, the knife in her hand pressing against his throat.

The goons were a split second too slow, though one tried anyway.

Dan fired, the shot catching him in the shoulder and spinning him around. The weapon dropped from his hand.

The other goon had his weapon halfway out when Dan turned to him.

"Don't," he said.

The bodyguard hesitated, looking toward St. Cyr.

"Tell him to drop it," Gemma suggested in the exact same tone she'd been using.

"Drop it," St. Cyr said. His pale gaze was on Gemma. He didn't look concerned.

"Clear," Dan said, when all weapons were out of their reach.

Gemma's arm lowered some, though she was still in striking distance.

"Kneel, hands clasped behind your heads," Dan ordered.

The bodyguards and the limo driver all did as they were told. The one he'd shot tried to do as he was told and cover his wound.

"You're going to have to clean that up," Abbot said.

Dan felt a grin tugging the edges of his mouth. St. Cyr hadn't moved. Maybe he thought his people were doing that for him?

"You should come work for me," St. Cyr said, looking at Gemma.

Dan hadn't thought he was offering him a job so he wasn't offended.

Gemma gave a chuckle and stood up. "You couldn't afford me."

"I beg your pardon?" St. Cyr actually looked kind of shocked.

Dan was surprised his face didn't crack from doing something it hadn't done in so long. If ever.

"I've seen your financials," Gemma said. She looked at the other men. "I hope he's not behind on your salaries."

All three men exchanged uneasy glances.

"I don't know why you'd think..." St. Cyr began.

"It's all those seizures by the Feds," she said. "Something your mother did?"

St. Cyr's fists clenched. "We'll leave my mother out of this."

"You started it," Gemma said. She bent to insert the knife back in the calf holster as a shot rang out.

St. Cyr had his second expression in as many minutes: a look of surprise as the impact of the shot flung him backward in the chair.

chapter twelve

Gemma felt a chill deep in her bones, despite the hot, bright sun beating down without mercy on a scene of organized chaos.

The *Reel Escape* swarmed with crime scene specialists and several types of law enforcement. She didn't know how they stood the heat in their protective gear.

Ruth seemed to be directing traffic on and off the boat while the tactical team stood to one side looking disappointed that the shooting was all over before they got there.

Shooting. She supposed she could use the phrase since it had been two shots fired. But it still felt like she was succumbing to drama.

The shot, the one that had killed St. Cyr felt like it had come really close to her. She'd swear she felt the air of it, or perhaps it was the heat, go by her head. Was that even possible? Or was her brain filling in postmortem data?

Who had that shot been meant for? St. Cyr had more enemies. The people who didn't like her didn't usually know she was the one who hosed them.

But this situation didn't seem to have anything to do with her job. If St. Cyr thought she knew where the wooden Rougarou was, perhaps someone else did, too?

143

But then…why try to kill her? It didn't make sense. Even in chaos she'd always been able to follow a logic line to a conclusion.

It was weird. While her mind replayed St. Cyr's death sprawl, she kept remembering how detached she'd felt all those years ago when they'd brought the bleeding man onto the *Reel Escape*.

She didn't feel detached this time, but it was also the first time someone had died in her presence.

She felt the tremor in her hands, though a glance assured her that clasped together like they were, the tremor didn't show.

But even weirder? She wasn't sure if Gemma or Shadow was in control. She felt…fractured. It was a weird sensation. She might be in shock.

She wanted to stretch out on a recliner and soak in the sun that her skin hated so much.

As if he realized it, Dan turned and called out something. In a minute an EMT had trotted over with one of those emergency blankets. Dan wrapped it around her and then rubbed her arms.

Without looking into her eyes, he said, "First time?"

She nodded, then realized he couldn't see it.

"Yes." Her voice surprised her by its steadiness. She wasn't sure who was more cautious when their gazes met. "Thank you," she added.

"This used to be my gig," he said. A smile briefly lightened his grim expression.

She tried to return it, but it felt sad from the inside. She wondered what it looked like on the outside.

"You did good," Dan said.

She gave a slight shake, not sure what he meant. She'd basically passed the buck—her handgun—to Dan. Seth wouldn't be happy with her.

"You hit the deck like a pro."

They'd all hit the deck. She felt a giggle trying to worm its way out because they'd literally hit the deck. It wasn't funny, but knowing that wasn't helping.

Was she getting hysterical? That would be so embarrassing.

"No more shots," she managed to get past the giggle. Did that mean St. Cyr was the target? "We didn't need to."

"We don't know that."

That was true.

"In the movies, there are always multiple shots." It kind of felt like the gunman had let them down.

"Welcome to reality," Dan said, his grin easier this time.

The smile warmed her more than the blanket. She wanted to lean into it, into him. So she wouldn't give into the temptation, she looked at the chaos.

"That all looks like the movies." Still without looking at him, she asked, "How did help arrive so fast?"

"Ruth was already assembling a team when I sent her a nine-one-one text."

"Backup is nice."

"That might be what scared the shooter off," Dan said. "They were closing in when the shots were fired."

Gemma tried not to sway, but she was close to out on her feet. All that adrenalin had drained away leaving her without reserves. She didn't notice Ruth approach, but Gemma lacked the strength to jump at the sound of her voice.

"They said we can sit in their tac van," Ruth said.

Dan gave her unobtrusive support both to it and getting inside.

It wasn't terribly cool, but it was a place to sit. From somewhere Dan produced a bottle of something. He removed the top and handed it to her.

"Electrolytes," he said. "Drink it all if you can."

Gemma sipped it, trying to organize the scene before her.

She mentally cordoned off the tac team, then sorted the various law enforcement groups by uniform. Little Abner was with one of those groups, gesticulating in fine form. He did love an audience.

There was an EMT unit providing some care to a delightedly shocked Ashley—who'd napped until the shots and possibly after.

"It will be fun getting her statement," Ruth observed.

"Let one of the local LEOs handle it," Dan said.

Gemma found she could smile more easily, though it set off a tremor in her arms. She clutched the blanket to her until it passed.

Little Abner looked around, saw them, and trotted over to join them. Dan extended a hand to him, and Little Abner took it, climbing and seating himself next to her.

"You okay?"

Gemma downed some more of the drink, wondering vaguely what flavor it was supposed to be.

"I'm fine," she said. She was recovering. It was inevitable, she supposed.

"Could someone tell me what happened?" Ruth asked. Her tone was far from interrogative, so it was interesting that Gemma felt suddenly wary.

Dan told his part of the story. "You managed to break the situation our way with your plan," he said to Little Abner.

"Don't know that I'd call it a plan," Little Abner said with unusual modesty. "I could tell he wouldn't believe I didn't know where his statue was."

"Figurine," Gemma corrected him absently. It was interesting to hear it from Dan's point of view, comparing it with her own as he talked.

"So they were actually looking for a Rougarou?" Ruth sounded amused and possibly a little bit stunned.

It was pretty ironic.

Ruth turned to her now. "So I'm assuming you have a permit for your weapon?"

"Yes, ma'am," she said promptly.

She waited for Dan to mention the knife, but he didn't. He'd asked her for it before the tac guys came on board. She'd unstrapped the holster and given both to him without a word of protest. She did hope he'd give it back. It was a good one. She'd had it a long time.

Her hand quivered again.

It was also the first time she'd held it against someone's throat.

She'd been close enough to see the pulse throbbing at St. Cyr's neck and his eyes had promised retribution.

He'd believed—probably rightly—that he'd be bailed out and able to exact that revenge.

She couldn't be sorry he was dead, she just wished she knew he was the one that bullet was meant for.

The shivers spread further up her arm, and she was once again glad for the blanket that hid her weakness.

She'd lived thirty-five years without anyone trying to kill her.

Was it the past bubbling up that had triggered this? Her instincts said it was all connected.

"And do you have the Rougarou?" Ruth asked, then twitched like it hadn't come out the way she intended. She saw Dan's lips twitch.

For the first time, she realized the adventure was probably over. She had the impression they thought St. Cyr had probably been behind both murders.

Did she believe it? She wasn't sure. On the other hand, it wasn't comfortable wondering if the woman who had given her life was the one behind trying to end it.

Was Mary Dailey truly still alive out there somewhere? Gemma felt no sense of connection, no longing to go find her. If she was alive, she'd ignored her all of her life. And if she wasn't, then what was the point of feeling dramatic about it?

She just wished she felt like the landmine had gone off. The bombshell she thought St. Cyr would set off had been kind of a dud—an amusing dud but still a dud.

She was aware that Ruth and Little Abner were talking, but she wasn't actually listening. That was kind of weird. Usually her brain could multi-task better. She still felt disconnected and floaty.

Dan leaned forward, his hands clasped in front of him mere inches from her knees. She wished she could touch him. It felt as if he'd bring her down gently.

He hadn't done it to touch her, she reminded herself. He was holding his own hands.

"Do you think St. Cyr was behind our two so-called Rougarou deaths?"

The question was direct, and so was his gaze fixed on her. The answer came from deep in her gut.

"No."

That yanked Ruth's attention her way.

"You don't?" Dan straightened.

"Why not?" Ruth asked, though her tone was close to a demand.

"I," Gemma hesitated, then finished, "I don't know. I just do, or don't? I don't think he was behind the deaths." She considered the question with an actual frown. She didn't even care if it was a giveaway. "He was late to the party," she finally said.

"We do have two other missing people," Ruth said. She exchanged a look with Dan, then they both turned their attention back to her and Little Abner. Mainly it was her, though.

"We only know the name of one of them," Dan said, his gaze not leaving her.

"Do you?" Gemma had a feeling they suspected Mary Bailey had been the one on that plane. They had to have found out about her.

"We have speculations and not much more," Ruth said.

Gemma decided she still liked her, even if she had suspected her of murder. Did Ruth still suspect her?

Gemma wasn't sure, but it didn't change the liking. Poor Little Abner. She couldn't see Ruth being interested in him. Poor me, her thoughts followed that one along the same path. Poor them. Neither Ruth or Dan would or could be interested in them.

It was probably a conflict of interest or something.

Dan hesitated. "We have facial recognition running on our…speculations."

So he was doing the search she couldn't bring herself to do.

"No results yet," he added, as if she'd asked.

"Will we be allowed back on the *Reel Escape* soon?" Little Abner asked.

Ruth shook her head and managed to look regretful. Possibly she really was.

"We'll escort you on board to collect some things and..." she didn't finish the sentence, as a frown formed on her face. Then she speared Gemma with a look. "Do you think that shot was meant for you?"

"I don't know," Gemma said. She really didn't. "I can't think why anyone would shoot me."

It had been a close call. She could make the case for someone taking the shot when St. Cyr was clear. And for someone taking the shot too late and hitting St. Cyr.

"There were plenty of people who wanted St. Cyr out of the picture," Dan said.

She wished he sounded more convinced. She wished she felt more convinced.

"Can I have my gun back?" She didn't want to be caught unarmed if someone was intent on killing her. Okay, just thinking that felt so weird.

"When I see your permit," Ruth said, after a long pause. Her gaze stabbed at Gemma again. "Who are you really?"

It surprised Gemma how much she wanted to answer that question.

It might be time to find another job.

* * *

Dan knew Gemma wouldn't answer. She'd already told him she couldn't. He wished she would anyway.

He wished...the thought got tangled with a weird and unfamiliar longing.

He could tell she was still suffering from shock. That was actually encouraging. It meant that, despite the weapons, she wasn't used to what had happened. This tracked with what he felt about her at an instinctive level. She was a good person. He was sure of it.

His instinct wouldn't be much help with Ruth.

"I need to make a phone call," she said finally.

She didn't make a promise that this would change anything, but he saw in her eyes that she wanted it to.

"What are they talking about, Gemma?" Abbot looked confused.

So he didn't know. That was interesting. And puzzling.

Gemma gave a half-smile that made his heart jerk.

"I'm allowed one phone call, aren't I?"

"You're not under arrest," Ruth said, "but yes, you can have your phone call. Do you need access to a phone?"

Gemma produced a cellphone from a pocket.

"I have my own."

Ruth didn't show it, but Dan knew she'd been hoping her phone had been misplaced by St. Cyr's goons so Gemma would have to use Ruth's phone.

He thought she'd excuse herself, but she didn't. It didn't take her long to dial, which meant the number was on her favorites' list.

There was a pause, and then they heard a phone ringing outside on the dock.

*   *   *

Gemma looked toward the sound. She even knew the ring.

She scooted to the end of the bench and looked out in the direction of the sound.

It was Seth. She shook her head as if to make sure she was awake.

He didn't fade. Instead, he answered her call, lifting the phone to his ear.

Gemma put her phone to her ear, too. "Look around you."

She tried to keep "you idiot" out of her tone. She wasn't sure she succeeded. Yeah, she really needed a new job.

She was aware that Dan slid up beside her, so he saw Seth look around and then see her.

He lifted a hand in that almost royal way and began making his way toward her.

Gemma didn't see Valka. That might surprise her. According to office gossip, she liked to travel with Seth to keep him from finding a younger assistant.

Seth reached the van, but didn't make a move to join them inside.

He wouldn't. Not his style at all.

"Gemma."

Gemma wasn't sure how to respond. She usually called him by his name, since that was all she knew, but she didn't know if he wanted his name floating around here right now.

"Sir."

His lashes flickered, then he glanced around and nodded. He was no slouch in the brains department.

She jumped down next to him, shedding the blanket and bundling it in her arms.

"This is Ruth Fossette, Dan Baker, and Abner Abbot, sir."

Dan and Ruth jumped down and presented their CGIS IDs. Little Abner stayed where he was, half in shadow Gemma noticed.

Seth didn't speak, so Gemma said, "This is my employer."

"Are you Smith or Jones?" Ruth asked.

Gemma's lips twitched. She'd wondered that, too.

"Smith," he said after a pause that ended a hair before it got too long.

"They need to know why a secretary for efficiency experts was carrying a licensed handgun," Gemma said. If she didn't goose things along they would be here fencing forever.

She was tired. She was hot. She was hungry. She felt sick, too.

If she was going to try eating, she needed to be where she could barf. By herself.

"Gemma works for the investigative arm of Smith and Jones," Seth said, putting on his easy charm persona that still managed to maintain a distance.

She watched Ruth and Dan to see what they made of him. Not much, she decided, with an inner grin. Seth may have found his match.

"She mentioned she was good at finding out things," Ruth said.

Gemma could tell Seth was processing this for possible violation of her non-disclosure agreement.

It wasn't. She knew right where the line was.

"Is Gemma in trouble?" Seth asked.

Was he worried? She couldn't tell. He hadn't called his side operation Enigma for no reason.

Ruth took her time answering. Strangely, this didn't worry Gemma. There was a certain power in knowing she hadn't done anything wrong.

"This situation is complicated, but no, she's not in legal trouble," Ruth said.

That was nice to hear.

"I'm glad to hear it—and not surprised. Gemma is one of the most ethical people I know."

Gemma blinked. Had she ever heard him give her more praise than a brief "good work?"

"She has become mixed up in some local trouble," Dan said.

"Perhaps Gemma could brief me," Seth said. He glanced around as if he expected a private space to pop up for his use. "Privately."

"We're not through taking her statement," Dan said.

There was enough of an edge in his tone, that she glanced at him. His expression was as bland as Seth's. There was a definite under current running between the two men though.

Gemma didn't frown because with Seth here, she had to go back to not using giveaway expressions.

She was suddenly sharply aware of the thick fishy smell coming off the canal. It came with traces of the spices from a nearby restaurant and the two men's competing aftershaves. Heat had a smell, too, or perhaps it was the things it heated up, like the asphalt.

No surprise a curious crowd had gathered around the edges, mostly fishermen and dock workers, she guessed. There were one or two people who didn't fit that slot. Tourists maybe? Did tourists find their way to Cocodrie?

The crime scene chaos was winding down. The various groups were gathering in and beginning to load their vehicles with what they'd collected. The number of vehicles began to thin.

Two men brought St. Cyr's covered body off the *Reel Escape* and loaded it into an ambulance.

Don't bring my mother into this, St. Cyr had said.

"Has anyone told his mother?" she asked. Even bad guys had next of kin.

The last time she'd seen his bodyguards and the limo driver, they'd been handcuffed and marched away. She didn't see them anywhere now. Would one of them use their one phone call to let her know?

"We'll have someone in New Orleans go talk to her," Ruth said.

They had to step aside as the tactical team came up and began loading their equipment into their van. Soon they'd take what little shade they had away.

She wanted to go away, too. But where could she go? Home was a crime scene. Her absent gaze slid over what was left among the onlookers. One of the men made her brain twitch. She tipped her head to the side, studying him and then realized he was looking at her.

She let her gaze drift up, above his head, and then away. It helped that Little Abner broke the stalemate between Dan and Seth.

"Can we get our stuff now?" he asked.

Ruth glanced between the two men, then said, "I'll take you."

As Gemma turned to follow them, she glanced in the man's direction, but he was gone.

chapter thirteen

After Gemma and Little Abner had retrieved their things, they all went to the Coast Guard station in an official airboat.

Dan hid a grin when the wind ruffled Seth's perfect hair. The guy almost didn't seem real. It was hard to wrap his brain around the fact that Gemma worked for him. But it also explained a lot of the inconsistencies he'd noticed about her.

They trooped into the station and were given the use of one of the meeting rooms. At least they were all out of the sun. By the time, they were all inside, Dan noticed Seth had smoothed his hair.

The room smelled stale, but he knew better than to open the window. He noted a stand fan and went over and turned it on. It helped a little.

Seth went to the head of the table.

It should have worked as a power position, but this wasn't his turf.

Little Abner sat next to Ruth. Dan gave him chops for hanging in there.

Gemma seemed preoccupied.

"Is something wrong?" he asked, taking a seat next to her.

She looked at him and gave a small shake of her head. "Could

I see the picture of the other missing guy? The pilot, I think you said?"

Dan dug into his jacket pocket and pulled out all the photos, shuffling through them for the Chester Milkens' photos. He handed them to her.

She stared at them both, one finger tapping the table.

"I think he was in the crowd back there," she said finally. She frowned down at the aged photo. "It could be him."

Dan's gaze met Ruth's. Perkins had been here so it was not a surprise to hear that Milkens might be here, too.

Dan felt unease spike in his gut. Could Milkens have been their shooter? The unknown woman was a wild card, too, though he didn't know how to look for her, since they didn't have much of a description.

Ruth rose. "I'll get the photo distributed locally and see if we get a hit."

Dan nodded. Was all this really about some wooden Rougarou? Could it be that valuable?

He knew Seth wanted to get Gemma alone. Dan didn't want that, though he wasn't sure why. Since he'd been with her, her statement was needed, but not urgently.

Dan might be impressed the guy showed no sign of impatience.

Ruth came back, stopping in the doorway as if the silence was a wall she couldn't push through.

"Mr. Smith," she said, "someone is here who says she's your personal assistant." She hesitated, looking uncomfortable, which was new to Dan. "Mr. Blaine is here, and he wants to talk to us."

Dan took a quick look at Gemma, but she was as much a sphinx as Seth, though she was more human about it.

He had to leave, but his feet dragged. He had to step back to let a scary old lady enter, the personal assistant he presumed.

"Valka," Seth said.

Dan felt his lips twitching as he went out. Of course her name was Valka. She looked like a mythical creature of some kind and not in a good way.

* * *

Who needed air conditioning when they had Valka?

Gemma nodded a greeting because that was all Valka did when her glance found Gemma and then slid past.

Little Abner looked a bit wide-eyed. He finally tore his gaze away and looked at Gemma, his white brows raised.

She shrugged. She was too busy trying to decide how she felt about her biological father being out there.

She'd known he existed for such a short time. And did she really believe those DNA results? Did she want to not believe them so she wouldn't have to deal with him?

She'd seen the movies and felt like she should care. Maybe she was in shock and that's why it felt like small potatoes? Even though it had turned out Fish wasn't her father, he was still her uncle and a blood relation. It gave her the sense of knowing "where she came from."

And then there was the fact that Fish had so rigorously hidden all this from her. Knowing Fish like she did—if she did?—he'd have had good reasons.

There was the will, she reluctantly recalled. Was it the real deal or a way for him to get his errant son under control? But...he could have picked anyone to twist up his heir.

She sighed. Blaine Senior sure hadn't rushed out to find her ten years ago.

The links were tenuous, but kind of there. The warehouse fire. The missing plane and people. Blaine, whose wife owned the warehouse. Her mother.

Four dead people.

It had to be about money.

St. Cyr needed money that the feds couldn't trace and seize.

Blaine needed money.

Perkins? She didn't know, but he either had the money or knew where it was. Thought he knew where it was? That could be it, too.

He and Blaine had been headed toward the same general area.

Could the missing figurine have even survived in the swamp for all these years? Just wondering that made her brain hurt.

Ledet and his pirogue? He could have been in on it or caught in the crossfire.

Oh my goodness. Her brain kind of stalled. She was acting like an amateur detective. It's had to stop.

She'd always meant to find a job where she could investigate animal and human interactions, i.e. animal attacks—did the critter or didn't it?

It was all more straight forward than man versus man. Less tangled than this swampy mess she found herself in.

She looked up and realized Seth and Little Abner were both staring at her.

"What?" She looked at one, then the other. "Did I miss something?"

"You're going to resign, aren't you?" Seth said.

It was a little creepy that he knew her that well, especially since she didn't really know him at all.

"Yes."

Valka's severe expression softened into something that might have been pleased.

Why didn't the woman like her? Gemma generally got along well with others. Other people at work liked her. Was there some kind of weird competition because Gemma started working with Seth before Valka?

Gemma tried to remember the personal assistant before Valka and couldn't. What had happened to her? Gemma knew her first sight of Valka, well, she tried to keep it, if not her last, then rare to look at her.

"I should have got here sooner." Seth looked resigned.

"It wouldn't have changed anything," Gemma said. Her gaze

met his and she had that same weird vibe she'd gotten the last time they met.

"You have no idea, do you?" Seth's thin mouth curved wryly as Gemma looked up in time to meet his gaze.

"I'm going to go with no," she said. It wasn't like her to lose the plot this badly, but she'd had a series of shocks, so she wasn't going to feel bad about it.

Valka had gone back to her pursed prune face.

"Perhaps it's just as well." He rose. "We need to get back."

She rose, too, not quite sure why. It wasn't as if they were going to hug or anything. She glanced down and realized Little Abner hadn't said anything. That was not like him.

"Little Abner? Are you all right?" she asked him and he jumped slightly.

She realized he had been staring at Valka. She hoped he wasn't going to try his luck there. He'd get frost bite.

The door opened, yanking her attention that way.

Dan stood in the opening, his gaze oddly anxious when it met hers. She had about half a second's realization before he stepped in, clearing the way for the man behind him.

It had to be Blaine Senior. He was an older version of Junior, but without the creepy vibes. If he was her bio-dad, that was one positive.

He stared at her and she had to resist the urge to shuffle her feet like she was back in grade school.

"Gemma." He cleared his throat. "You are very like your, um, mother."

He gave a start that may have signaled he didn't realize she wasn't alone. His gaze found Little Abner and passed on to Seth, then reached Valka and stopped, a puzzled frown forming between his brows.

To Gemma's surprise, Valka's face, well, it kind of melted into something almost human. Her chin lifted as if she hoped to brazen it out, then she sighed.

"Hello, Ray.'

"Mary?" He still looked puzzled. "You've had some work done."

"Apparently, not enough," Valka said.

Gemma turned and walked out of the room.

* * *

Dan followed Gemma out.

It looked like she'd found her landmine.

He caught up to her and took her hand.

She gave him a startled look, as if she hadn't realized he was there. But her hand returned his clasp.

"I'll bet you're hungry," he said.

Her eyes widened and then she nodded.

"I'm so hungry."

Should he be relieved her tone was calm? He was out of his depth here, acting on instinct.

They ended up back at the same place they'd eaten before, even ended up at the same table.

They examined their menus and ordered. Her hands were clasped in front of her, resting on the cheap tablecloth. Her lashes hid her eyes and her thoughts.

He wished someone better at this than he was were here. He hesitated, then reached across and covered her hands with his.

They were cold. He began to massage them, hoping to warm them, to warm her.

Her lashes lifted and she smiled.

"Well, that was a kick in the pants."

He was surprised when he chuckled, even more surprised when she did, too.

"Good thing I'd resigned before that bomb went off."

"You did?" He was ridiculously happy about that.

"I'd decided before I left. I was going to tell S—him then, but it just got a little weird and I left."

"That's because he likes you," Dan said. Apparently it was

hard to use the l-word no matter who it applied to. He blinked. L-word?

He examined himself for panic and found...none. So he might l-word her? His grip tightened.

"S—Mr. Smith?" She looked so startled and then she chuckled again and shook her head. "No way."

"He's never..." Dan wasn't sure what or how to ask it.

"The only time he's touched me was when he hired me and shook my hand. He stayed on his side of his big desk, and I stayed on the other. There was never..." she gave a small, almost shudder.

"So you don't..." he shouldn't press, but he needed to know.

"I've sometimes wondered if he was a vampire," she said. "But no, not now, not ever. He's just, or he was just my boss."

Her gaze was a little shy, but also less guarded than it had been—something he only realized now when she stopped doing it.

"Your hands are warming up." His voice was husky.

"Are they?" She glanced down, but only for a second.

"What," he had to clear his throat, "will you do now?"

"I always used to think I'd work for a park or something, investigating animal attacks."

He smiled. He couldn't help it. It surprised him that it didn't surprise him. She was unlike anyone he'd ever met.

"You should come work with Ruth and I," he said. Did he have the right to say it? He wasn't sure, but he knew he could make the case.

"You mean be a real investigator?" She looked thoughtful.

At least she didn't reject him out of hand.

"Yes." He was quiet for a moment. "It might be complicated."

"Complicated?"

"I lo—" he couldn't get the big commitment word out, so he said instead, "like you. I like you a lot."

"You do?"

Was she really surprised?

"You're amazing." How could she not know it? "A keeper," he added, edging as close to the commitment line as he dared. Did she like him?

The smile slowly spread across her face, spreading warmth through his body in a way he'd never experienced before.

She was beautiful, like a jewel that only sparkled for him. She'd been hiding in the shadows. He felt a flicker of something because Mr. Smith had seen it, but she had left him, he reminded himself. He felt certain she'd never smiled like this for him.

"I like you, too. And complications don't scare me."

Did anything? She'd stayed so cool-headed during the whole incident with St. Cyr. And then left when her parents showed up, but that was totally natural. He loved Zach, but he'd been hiding from him for almost a year now.

"Will you come and meet my family?" It was time to man up. And she'd be a great distraction from his failure to mention his change of career.

"Meet your family?"

"Is it too soon?"

Now she grinned. "Well, it can't be any worse than my family reunion."

He nodded like it was true. It was possible, though he'd never say never where his family was concerned.

Someone approached their table and Dan looked that way, expecting it to be their food. That's right, they had come here to eat.

It wasn't the server.

The man was older and vaguely familiar. Before Dan could place him, he sat down next to him and shoved a gun into his side.

"Chester Milkens, I presume," Gemma said.

*** * * ***

Dan met Gemma's gaze and he mouthed the word, "Gun."

"Let's not make a scene," Milkens said.

There was a blur of motion from across the table and she heard her third shot—was it her third shot—of the day.

This time it wasn't close. She had a feeling it thudded into the ceiling.

And then Dan had the gun.

"I like making scenes," Dan said.

The other patrons looked around curiously but not with a lot of alarm. A few had leaned forward, their hands on their own weapons. She had a feeling shootings happened from time to time here.

Just in case the patrons weren't sure who was the good guy, Dan showed his ID and then cuffed Milkens. He handed Gemma his cellphone.

"Could you call Ruth?"

She could and did. When she'd handed Dan his phone back, she told Milkens, "Your timing is terrible."

She looked over her shoulder and saw their server coming with their food. At least they hadn't got ceiling dust in their food.

* * *

Gemma had more color in her face after eating, Dan noted. He made Milkens sit handcuffed to a chair and watch them eat while they waited for Ruth.

He'd ruined the moment. Even his advanced age didn't earn him any points today.

He heard the sounds of multiple cars and maybe one siren. He took his eyes off Milkens for a minute to say, "I'm here for you. You know, with whatever."

He got another one of her amazing smiles as his reward.

"How did you get the gun?" She asked.

"I have six brothers," he said. Her eyes widened. So did Milkens. "And six sisters."

Milkens snorted. "That explains a lot."

chapter fourteen

It was a relief to be back on the *Reel Escape*. Mostly, Gemma conceded. It felt like there were a bunch of small landmines all over the deck—as if the big one going off had just scattered more crap for her to deal with, but without totally exploding.

That was an interesting thought. She half frowned. Had the mom bombshell really been a bombshell? It hadn't been a big enough bang to rearrange her world that much. Maybe she'd been expecting something bad for so long, she'd set her expectations low enough for the bang to just be a stiff breeze?

It was possible.

Only there was this sense of more crap incoming.

She walked to the railing, hoping to catch a stray breeze off the water. She was aware that Little Abner had followed up and out onto the deck.

Two incompatible thoughts bounced against each other inside her head.

Little Abner had stated more than once that he'd never met her birth mother.

It had seemed to her that Little Abner had recognized Valka before Blaine Senior came in.

One of these "truths" was not like the other one. The *Sesame Street* tune played idly in her head.

Maybe he hadn't known Valka as Gemma's birth mother? But that left the question of where and when he had seen her—and had enough time to feel a sense of recognition?

There was only one way to find out and that was only if Little Abner was finally willing to come clean.

She turned, propping her back agains the railing and regarded him from under the wide, floppy brim of her hat. She hadn't donned sunglasses because she knew she'd need her gaze on board for this moment.

"Yes, I recognized her," Little Abner admitted. He sank down on the end of a recliner and rubbed his face with his hands. "I did not know she was…" His voice trailed off.

"My birth mother?"

He nodded. "You need to know it all, I guess?"

"Was that a question?" She tipped her head to one side. "Because if it was, then the answer is yes. I need to know it all."

She crossed over and sank onto the end of the recliner next to his. She didn't use power plays that often, but she did know what they looked like, and this wasn't the time for that.

"Fish, Mary and I, well," he gave her a sidelong look, "were partners."

Partners. Gemma considered the word carefully, sensing many layers of nuance in the choice.

"Fish was a genius for figuring things out and Mary? She was smart, too, but she had a reckless streak and enough brass for fifty guys." Now Little Abner stared straight ahead. "I had a knack for moving…merchandise."

The light bulb had been flickering but now it lit up. "You were a fence."

He nodded uncomfortably. This admission clarified what the other two did. A little more clarity than she actually wanted for her genetic donors, she realized somewhat wryly.

"I got tired of it. I was closer to," he hesitated.

"The police end of things."

He nodded. "I grew up in Montana and had always dreamed

of living on the water, so I moved on, moved south and began working for different people, learning the ropes. This was maybe five years before you came along."

She'd wondered how he'd gone from fence to old sea dog, though she'd been young for a lot of those years.

"I don't know that much about what happened after I left, but Fish showed up one day and said he was done, too. He was over it. I figured he and Mary'd had a falling out. They'd always argued."

So Little Abner had known them that well clear back then. That was interesting. She sensed her own detachment from the story and realized it did feel like it had happened to people she didn't know.

This was uncomfortably true. She'd known who they became, not who they were. In a weird way, that was pretty typical of kids and their parents.

"Then Fish said he had business to attend to, not that kind of business," Little Abner added, "he knew I wouldn't put up with that reaching out to touch my the new life I'd built for myself."

Little Abner was silent for a minute or two, as if remembering, or trying to remember.

"I wondered if it had to do with Mary, but when he came back he had you and he told me you were the product of a fling he'd had." Little Abner rubbed his chin. "He had been gone at the relevant time, so I didn't think much of it."

"Weren't you taken aback?" Gemma asked.

"Well, yes. I wasn't sure how we'd manage it, but we did."

He didn't say why, but she thought she knew. The one certainty in her life was knowing they'd both loved her.

"Were you in love with her?" Gemma wasn't sure where the question came from.

"Everyone who met her was until…"

"Until they realized she didn't have a heart?"

Little Abner looked at her and then nodded slowly. "She was a little bit broken in that way. It took us all a while to understand and just get out of the disaster zone."

Well, that explained Valka's coldness to her at Enigma. She might wonder how she'd wandered across Seth's path, but did she really want to know that?

Everyone who met her was...

Yeah, that was better to never know.

"She came back one last time and gave something to Fish to keep for her. He didn't like it, but she had some kind of hold over him," he made a grimace, "now I know what it was. So he kept it for her."

"He kept it for her? But..." Gemma frowned.

Little Abner sighed heavily. "I pretty much lied to everyone about that."

"Where is it?" How far had he been willing to go to hold onto the secret? Of course, Dan had been there. She needed to find out what the statute of limitations was for theft.

"Here." Maybe he realized what she was thinking. "If it had been the only way, I'd have given it up, but they weren't going to let us go."

It was true. St. Cyr couldn't have afforded to leave witnesses behind. It had made it easier to act, knowing they'd die if she didn't act.

He rose and left, presumably going to get whatever it was that Mary had left here. Gemma slid back so she was stretched out on the recliner, considering all she'd learned.

There were gaps, but she could sort of fill them. Mary had presumably made a move on Blaine Senior to get close to whatever it was she wanted to steal. And had managed to get too close —or get careless with her birth control.

Considering when she'd been born, Mary could've had an abortion. That she hadn't might ease whatever sting Gemma felt. Of course, Fish could have found out and he had a hold over her, too. So she could probably let any warm and fuzzy feelings slide away.

That was a relief. Gemma didn't know anything about Mary the birth mother, but she knew enough about Valka to not want to show any weakness around her—assuming she ever saw her again.

Little Abner returned carrying a box. It was clearly an old box. He set it down at the feet she moved aside. She sat up as he produced a key and unlocked it. She leaned forward as he opened the lid.

The bundle of fabric had yellowed with age and some of it crumbled away when Little Abner pulled it back to reveal...

"The Rougarou," Gemma said. There was no question what it had been carved to be, though a case could be made for it being a werewolf, which was fitting. The wood was beautiful and smooth to the touch when she picked it up.

It was a hideously lovely piece but was it truly worth so many lives and effort? She was no art expert.

It was interesting that it was one of the few fields of study that had never interested her. Maybe she'd heard too much in the womb?

Her fingers ran over it, as she followed her instincts. It took her three passes before she found it. There was a click and the figurine split into two pieces, releasing a shower of white gems into her lap.

* * *

"I told Gemma she should come work with us," Dan said, keeping his eyes on the screen and the report he was typing in. He didn't let the long silence distract him.

"She's good," Ruth admitted. "Can you keep the personal complications out of work?"

Dan considered this. "I did it on the boat."

The Coast Guard had regulations, but Gemma was a civilian. He was pretty sure Ruth would know a workaround if she wanted Gemma.

And if she didn't?

Well, he'd changed careers once. Maybe they could go work for Gideon as private detectives. Or start their own agency. With a start he realized how long term he was thinking.

He shouldn't be that surprised. One of the reasons he'd avoided going home was all that happiness reminded him he was alone. He was tired of it. He loved his Triumph, but it didn't keep him warm at night or smile at him like Gemma.

She'd look good sitting pillion with him. He let himself dwell on that while Ruth worked through her thoughts.

"You already asked her, didn't you?"

Gideon finally turned to meet her gaze. "I did," he admitted, "but she didn't give me an answer."

"Well, I hope she doesn't take as long as you did to decide."

Dan grinned. He couldn't argue with her. But he did have, he hoped, some extra persuasions to bring to the table. If he hadn't misread her smiles. And he didn't think he had.

chapter fifteen

Gemma had no idea what to do with the diamonds—if they were diamonds. But if they were, it explained so much. And it was, she admitted to herself, a relief there was a Rougarou, but not a *Rougarou* in all this.

It also explained the slash marks on the bodies. They were sending a message.

She paced slowly around the deck, noticing a storm building out in the Gulf. At least it was just nature kicking up a fuss, and no one messing in her life anymore.

Being here, being on the *Reel Escape,* felt different. She was different, she decided. It wasn't just falling into…like…with Dan. It was more than that. And it wasn't about her biological parents either. She almost snorted.

She went over to the recliner and stretched her legs out, the rising humidity of the coming storm too much for pacing.

She wore her usual sun protection clothes, including her big hat and sunglasses.

The warmth felt good though, it had since, well, everything.

She reached for her laptop and opened it up. It was time to make it official with Seth, just in case he was holding out hope.

For just a moment, she considered what Dan had said about Seth liking her, but then she shook it off. She'd had to deal with enough weird this week to last her a lifetime. She couldn't go there, even in her thoughts.

She opened the company portal and there was a message waiting for her from Seth.

Are you okay?

Did you know, she typed back.

There was a pause and then *NO.*

Wow, that was emphatic for Seth.

I'm fine.

She was mostly fine. She hadn't seen Valka or Blaine and that helped. She'd thought about demanding proof, DNA tests she could supervise, but then she realized she didn't need or want proof.

Donating genetic material didn't make either of them a parent. Fish, for all his eccentricities, not to mention the secrets he'd withheld, had been her father and her mother. Or maybe Little Abner had been the mom.

This thought made it easier her for to adjust to what she'd learned. She was not giving up on the last member of her real family. If she did say, marry someone with dreamy eyes and a killer smile, she needed someone to give her away.

As for Valka, she'd had more chances than she deserved. Gemma would be perfectly happy for her to leave her life forever.

Valka or Mary or whatever she wanted to call herself, wasn't going to leave without the Rougarou, of course, even if she had to steal it back. Idly Gemma wondered if she had tried. That had to be some good hiding place Fish or Little Abner had created.

She and Little Abner had talked about it—and kind of sideways about Mary and the Rougarou.

St. Cyr was dead. Anyone else possibly involved was either dead or in jail. Except for Mary.

Gemma had eyed Little Abner and realized there was just a tiny bit of feeling left in his heart for Mary.

"Give it to her," she said. Little Abner hadn't asked who "she" was. He'd just gathered the stones up and put them back in the figurine. And Gemma had put it back together.

Gemma had to be the one to send the text, since she had her phone number. Little Abner had left with the figurine and just a hint of a smile on his face.

Maybe he'd get some closure. And get over Ruth at the same time.

Mary or Valka hadn't even bothered to respond.

That pretty much said it all as far as Gemma was concerned.

And Blaine had known for ten years and kept his distance.

If she owed either of them thanks, it would be for that, for staying out of her life.

She examined the spot in her, the place where the landmine had lived in her since that day with Fish.

It was gone.

She touched her chest tentatively, then rubbed the spot. Yup, it was gone.

Her mind was quiet, too. The questions had settled down, some had faded, and the ones she had? Well, they revolved around Dan at the moment. But they weren't anxious questions. She was surprised in her quiet confidence that he'd show up when he'd cleared his decks.

She gave a sigh of relief, closed her laptop and leaned back. She could resign later. If Seth hadn't already shut her out of the portal and taken her off the payroll. He didn't mess around.

She heard a sound and looked up.

Dan was standing there looking down at her with a smile that made her heart literally turn over in her chest.

Looked like he didn't mess around either.

epilogue

Gemma eyed the gleaming motorcycle, a Triumph Bonneville, according to Dan. It did look amazing.

"I've never ridden on a motorcycle," she admitted.

Dan looked up, from where he knelt by the bike tweaking something or other.

"You'll love it," he said.

Speeding along the highway, forced to hug Dan tightly? What wasn't to love about it?

Dan's gaze ran lightly over her and then he smiled his appreciation.

"You dressed for it."

Of course she had. It had been super easy to research biker babe gear. She couldn't say she'd loved the leather in these temperatures, but the look in Dan's eyes helped.

And knowing they were heading up to New Orleans to meet Dan's family helped provide a nice chill.

It helped some, knowing he'd met her "family" and hadn't bolted into the sunset.

She hadn't asked Little Abner how the meeting with Valka/Mary went and he hadn't tried to tell her.

The air had finally cleared on the *Reel Escape*. All the landmines had been exploded or defused. Little Abner had been unsurprised by her announcement that she was going to New Orleans with Dan.

He knew she wasn't leaving him forever, just as she knew he'd be there when and how he could, for as long as he could. He'd have to live long enough to give her away.

She flinched inside at this thought. She was assuming a lot from a guy who'd only used the "like" word and not the "love" word.

She studied his leather covered back, wondering why she trusted him. She should totally have trust issues with her past and present. Mountains of trust issues. And some swamps, too.

He rose and dusted his hands on a rag he'd draped across the seat. He smiled at her, his eyes gleaming with a lot more than like.

Would she know that? It felt like she knew that.

"Ready?" He asked.

She nodded. "So how do we do this?"

He held out his hand. He hadn't donned the heavy gloves yet, so his clasp was both comforting and thrilling.

"I'll show you," he said.

* * *

Thank you for reading *Pirogue Wipe Out!* I hope you enjoyed reading it as much as I enjoyed writing it! Stay tuned for the next book in the series: *Bourre Brouhaha* releasing November 17, 2022!

Here's a short blurb:

Eddie Baker is a firefighter.

Audrey Goodheart is the daughter of an arsonist.

What could possibly go wrong?

Bourre Brouhaha releasing November 17, 2022!

Pirogue Wipeout

THE BIG UNEASY BOOK EIGHT
Bourré Brouhaha

acknowledgments

I couldn't have finished this book without the love and support of my family.

And it wouldn't be as good without Alexis Glynn Latner and Amy Brantley.

And finally, I am so grateful for the amazing encouragement of Narelle Todd and Get My Book There (and the GMBOT gals!).

Thank you to all of you and to my amazing readers.

also by pauline baird jones

Romantic Suspense

The Big Uneasy Series:
Relatively Risky (1)
Family Treed (A Big Uneasy Short Story)
Dead Spaces (2.0)
Louisiana Lagniappe (3.0)
Worry Beads (4.0)
Fais Do Do Die (5.0)
Beaucoup Fracas (6.0)
Pirogue Wipe Out (7.0)
Bourre Brouhaha (8.0)
The Family Way (A Big Uneasy Short Story)
The Big Uneasy Bundle
An Uneasy Collection: The Big Uneasy Books 3-5

Lonesome Lawmen Series:
The Last Enemy
Byte Me
Missing You
Lonesome Mama (Bonus short story)
(The *Lonesome Lawmen* is also available as a digital bundle)

Do Wah Diddy Die
The Spy Who Kissed Me
Perilously Fun Fiction Bundle (includes *The Spy Who Kissed Me* and *Do Wah Diddy Die*. Bonus: *Do Wah Diddy Delete Short Story Collection*)

Dangerous Dance

A Dangerous Duet - 2024

Science Fiction Romance/Paranormal

Project Universe Series:

The Key (book 1)

Girl Gone Nova (book 2)

Tangled in Time (book 3)

Steamrolled (book 4)

Kicking Ashe (book 5)

Found Girl (book 6)

Lost Valyr (book 7)

Maestra Rising (book 8)

Cosmic Boom (book 9)

Project Enterprise: The Short Stories

Time Trap: A Project Enterprise Series Short Story

Operation Ark: A Project Enterprise Story

Cyborg's Revenge: A Project Enterprise Story.

General's Holiday: A Project Enterprise Story

Claws & Effect: The Otherworldly Pets of Project Enterprise

CabeX: A Project Enterprise Story

The Real Dragon

Nebula Nine (time travel adventure)

Open With Care (Christmas collection that includes, "Riding For Christmas" and "Up on the House Top"

Specters in the Storm: A paranormal/steampunk/science fiction romance novella

Out of Time (World War II Time Travel Romance)

Just in Time (An Out of Time Story)

An Uneasy Future

(A science fiction romance mystery series set in future New Orleans)

Core Punch (1.0)

Sucker Punch (2.0)

One Two Punch: An Uneasy Future Bundle

Short Story Collections

Project Enterprise: The Short Stories

Do Wah Diddy Delete

Let's Fall in Love

Take a Chance on Me

The Real Dragon and other short stories

about the author

Award-winning, *USA Today* Bestselling author Pauline never liked reality, so she writes books. She likes to wander among the genres, rampaging like Godzilla, because she does love peril mixed in her romance.

To find out more about Pauline or her books:
http://paulinebjones.com

Made in the USA
Middletown, DE
23 September 2022